FLYING WING: a group of three or four aircraft squadrons

You can't let the haters get you down, Viva.

HYPOTHERMIA: hy·po·ther·mi·a /ˌhīpəˈTHərmēə/
the condition of having an abnormally low body temperature, typically one that is dangerously low

What's a logophile? It's a person who loves words.

SHENANIGANS: she·nan·i·gans /SHəˈnanəgənz/
silly or high-spirited behavior; mischief

Supremeness

MESS: An acronym for MAINTENANCE OF EQUAL SOCIAL STATUS. The goal of the MESS is to maintain equal social status amongst all its members, irrespective of their rank.

Wings to
SOAR

Wings to SOAR

Tina Athaide

CHARLESBRIDGE
MOVES

Soar on over to the webpage for *Wings to Soar* for additional content. You can put together a puzzle of Viva's journey and more! Visit **www.charlesbridgemoves.com/WingstoSoar** or scan this QR code.

Published by Charlesbridge Moves, an imprint of Charlesbridge Publishing
9 Galen Street, Watertown, MA 02472
(617) 926-0329 • www.charlesbridgemoves.com

Library of Congress Cataloging-in-Publication Data
Names: Athaide, Tina, author.
Title: Wings to soar / Tina Athaide.
Description: Watertown, MA: Charlesbridge, [2024] | Audience: Ages 10–12 |
    Audience: Grades 4–6 | Summary: In 1972 Viva and her Indian family were forced
    to leave Uganda—now in a resettlement camp in England she struggles to cope
    with the living conditions there, hoping that her father may join them soon.
Identifiers: LCCN 2023017273 (print) | LCCN 2023017274 (ebook) |
    ISBN 9781623544317 (hardcover) | ISBN 9781632893901 (ebook)
Subjects: LCSH: Refugees—Uganda—Juvenile fiction. | Refugees—Great Britain—
    Juvenile fiction. | Forced migration—Uganda—Juvenile fiction. | Refugee camps—
    England—Greenham (West Berkshire)—Juvenile fiction. | Uganda—History—
    1971–1979—Juvenile fiction. | Greenham (West Berkshire, England)—History—
    20th century—Juvenile fiction. | CYAC: Refugees—Fiction. | Forced migration—
    Uganda—Fiction. | Refugee camps—Fiction. | Uganda History—1971–1979—
    Fiction. | Greenham (West Berkshire, England)—Fiction. | Great Britain—
    History—20th century—Fiction. | LCGFT: Autobiographical fiction.
Classification: LCC PZ7.1.A887 Wi 2024 (print) | LCC PZ7.1.A887 (ebook) |
    DDC [Fic]—dc23
LC record available at https://lccn.loc.gov/2023017273
LC ebook record available at https://lccn.loc.gov/2023017274

Printed in China
(hc) 10 9 8 7 6 5 4 3 2 1

Illustrations done in acrylic paint, cut paper, and tissue paper on illustration board
Display type set in October Story by Sronstudio
Text type set in Tekton by Adobe Systems Incorporated
Printed by 1010 Printing International Limited in Huizhou, Guangdong, China
Production supervision by Mira Kennedy
Designed by Diane M. Earley

Thank you Graham Jewell and to the officers and volunteers at Greenham Common Resettlement Camp for their service and kindness—T. A.

Thank you to Andrea Cascardi, Eileen Robinson, Diane Earley, Mira Kennedy, Natalia Vázquez Torres, Jonathan Sayers, Kayla Penney, and Bella Shannon for seeing what this book could be and laboring over every word, and thanks to illustrator London Ladd for bringing Viva to life.

A very special thanks to Alexandra McKenzie for seeing Viva's worth in the world and bringing her story to acquisitions.

DREAMS

Hold fast to dreams
For if dreams die
Life is a broken-winged bird
That cannot fly.

Langston Hughes

October 1972

I.
Have.
A.
Name.

Who am I?

I am a refugee.

RE-FU-GEE

That's what
they
call me,
the workers in the resettlement camp,
the newspaper journalists,
the television reporters,
the Prime Minister, and
the picketers with their angry signs.

They call me the REFUGEE from Uganda!

I want to shout

I.
Have.
A.
Name.

It's not refugee!

It's Viva!

Viva

My name
fits me
perfectly.

Daddy says
eleven years ago
I came rushing
into this world,
and leaped
right into my life.

Mummy says
I started singing
the minute I was born.

That's when they decided
to name me Viva.

It means
     alive,
     spirited,
     living life.

        ME!

I was almost Irene.
That name is
for someone
peaceful
and quiet.

Can you believe it?
Irene.
        BLAH.

But refugee is worse.
I **hate** it!

What does refugee mean?

When I want
to know more about a word
Daddy gets out the *Oxford Dictionary*.
Time for Big Blue.
Then he starts singing . . .

A-hunting we will go.
A-hunting we will go.
Undeterred, we'll find the word,
A-hunting we will go.

And the search begins.
We hunt
through the pages
until we find the word.
It's our thing.

Sometimes my sister,
Anna, helps.
She's super-duper fast
at finding words,
but usually disappears back
into whatever book
she's reading,
which is fine
because I
like it better
when it's just
Daddy and me.

The search
will be harder
this time.

Big Blue isn't here.

Neither is Daddy.

5

RAF Greenham

Daddy is
in our house
on the seven hills
in Kampala,
Uganda.

Miles and miles away.

I'm with
Mummy and Anna
in a camp
surrounded by
other Indians,
American soldiers,
English people,
and looming gray skies.

RAF Greenham
in England.
An old military base
being used
by the Americans.
RAF
The Royal Air Force.

Miles and miles away
from anything Royal
like Queen Elizabeth,
Prince Philip,
and Buckingham Palace.

Miles and miles away
    from Daddy,
    from Big Blue.

HELP!

Mummy and Anna
have been taken over
        by GLOOM.

All the sun
has been
squeezed out
of them
and there's
nothing
left but
    sadness.

It's up to me
to spark
the sunshine
and keep it lit
until Daddy
gets here.

I know
just what to do.
We'll hunt
for Big Blue together.
It always makes
Daddy and me

    SMILE.

Mummy won't budge.

I'm going to the common hall.
Will you come with me?
    Not today.

Please.
Mummy firmly
shakes her head
and pats my hand.
    Maybe tomorrow,
she says.

This
is going to be
much harder
than I thought.

Mummy's gloom
is as thick
and gray
as the storm clouds
hanging in the sky.

Anna is GLOOM and DOOM.

I'm going to the common hall.
Come with me.   *No.*

I want to look up a word
and you can find them
faster than me.   *I'm reading.*

You're always reading.
Come on.
I don't want to go alone.   *It's cold and*
                                        the air is bad
                                        for my lungs.

It's not far and we'll go quickly.
Daddy will be here in five days
and we can surprise him with
new words.   *Nobody cares*
                                        about your
                                        new words.
                                        They're stupid!

You're stupid!

Outside

I stomp out
of the barracks
with only
myself
for company.

In Kampala
I had loads
of friends
and my
best friend, Ella.
Here
I'm
alone.

The sky pours
and the icy rain
feels like tiny needle pricks
on my skin.

I hate
when Anna
uses her *breathing*
to get out
of doing stuff.

She rushed
into her life
a month too early
so her lungs
need time
to catch up.

She's eleven.
A year older than me.
How much catching up time
do her lungs need?

Rain trickles
inside my too-big
borrowed coat
that doesn't
fit right.

I dash around
the red brick building.

Down
    Down
        Down
            the hill.

Past
smiling soldiers,
scowling Englishmen,
waving English volunteers,
serious police officers,
straight into the
                L O N G building.

The Common Hall

The common hall
is for Indians
to hang out,
play table tennis and cards,
listen to records,
catch up on news.

I miss
our club
in Kampala.

It was filled with
Music
Singing
Dancing
Chatter
Laughter.

The common hall
is empty today.
Quiet,
except for
my chattering teeth
and squeaky
too-big rubber boots.

In the far corner
is the library.
Books
Magazines
Newspapers.
And hopefully, an *Oxford Dictionary*.

An English Big Blue.

The Women's Royal Volunteer Service

WRVS women are everywhere.
Volunteering.
Helping.

The two Robinsons
run the library.
Old Mrs. Robinson,
    Frosty.
    Growling.
    Cranky.
And her niece,
young Miss Robinson,
    Sparkly.
    Chatty.
    Friendly.

Who will be there today?

No one can stop me.

I sashay
like Diana Ross
singing . . .

> This cold and rain.
> This dreary place
> Won't stop me.

I sing to
the tune of . . .

> "Ain't No Mountain High Enough"

switching out
Diana's words for
my own.

It's our song.
The song
Ella and I picked
before she left me.
Before I
left Daddy.

It's our HOPE song.

Today,
nothing's going
to stop me
from finding
a dictionary.

Nothin's gonna stop me
from finding youuuuuu . . .

            SHHH!

All my Diana supremeness
is BLOCKED
by Old Mrs. Robinson.
Quiet! And no running, young lady.

   Nothin's gonna stop me
   from finding youuuuuu . . .

I whisper
and fast-walk
to the rows
of books.
Then stop.

He's here.

The Boy

Blond hair
Freckly nose
Squinty blue eyes

Every time
I come to
the library
he's here.
Sorting.
Straightening.
Organizing.
Like he owns
the place.
He sure seems
to know
where everything goes.

Have you seen an *Oxford Dictionary?*
I ask.

He looks up.
Startled.
Quickly shoves the books
on the shelf
and rushes off.

How rude!
But he's gone,
so there's nobody
trailing me.
Sorting.
Straightening.
Organizing.

A-hunting I will go . . .

16

Mini Blue

I search
through the stacks
for the blue spine
and gold lettering.

Nothing

I keep looking
until there's
only one shelf left.

PLEASE BE HERE.

Hidden in the corner
I spot it.
It's the size
of sandwich bread,
but thicker.

The Little Oxford Dictionary

Mini Blue.

Refugee

It takes me
longer
without Daddy,
but I find the word
on page 482
between the two headwords
reflective and regale.

REFUGEE: ref·u·gee /ˌrefyùˈjē/
a person who has been forced to leave their country or home,
because there is a war or for political, religious, or social reasons

I say the word slowly.

RE . . . FU . . . GEE.

Each syllable
feels like raw mango
on my tongue.

Bitter.

Nasty.

Unwanted.

Boy Has a Sister

I'm
writing
the definition
in my word book
but some
annoying girl
is clicking her tongue
and tapping her toes.

I aim
my best
knock-it-off glare.
She grins.

No way!
It's Boy
with long hair
and a dress.

I look away
super fast.
But not fast enough.
She rushes over
and now
she is standing . . .

Right In

Front Of

Me!

Maggie Mackay

Hello.
I'm Maggie.
Maggie Mackay.
What's your name?
Where's that other girl?
Is she your sister?
You're from Uganda, aren't you?
What are you writing?

She doesn't
take a breath.
Just shoots questions
one
after
the
next.

My head spins.

I have a twin brother, Mark.
He didn't like you moving the books.
You scared him.

And then
she breaks into
a way-too-high giggle.
I join her
and we giggle together.

It feels good.

There's not been much
to laugh
about lately.

Mark Mackay

Mark always
starts his sentences
with . . .
        Did you know that—
And then
just like Maggie,
he spews words,
only his are full
of facts and tidbits.

He is a
walking
talking
living
breathing
encyclopedia, dictionary, and newspaper
all rolled
into an eleven-year-old brain.

He knows interesting stuff,
but sometimes
I wish
he'd shut up.

I'd never
tell him that.
But Maggie does.
She groans and says,

Oh, for the love of God and all that is almighty,
    would
        you
           just
               SHUT UP!

The MESS

When the smiling lady
took us
to the MESS hall
on our first day
in the camp,
I imagined

A GREAT GINORMOUS MESS

But it wasn't.
It was a food hall.
And it wasn't
messy.

At supper last night
Mark told me
MESS
is an acronym.
Daddy will like the word
so I added it
to my book.

> **MESS**: An acronym for MAINTENANCE OF EQUAL SOCIAL
> STATUS. The goal of the MESS is to maintain equal social
> status amongst all its members, irrespective of their rank.

(Note to Daddy: I didn't find this definition in Mini Blue.)

Fish and Chips

It's the same smell
every time I walk
into the MESS hall.

Earthy cumin.
Bitter turmeric.
Warm cinnamon.
Pungent garlic and ginger.

The volunteer ladies
try and get me
to eat
orangey chicken curry,
with mounds of rice,
or soupy dal.

But there's
only one thing
I want . . .

FISH AND CHIPS!

Crispy, battered fish.
Fat, potatoey chips.
Mushy green peas
swimming in butter. YUM!

I've eaten it
at lunch and dinner
for the past two days
and plan
on eating it
until Daddy arrives
and we
leave for Canada.

Miss Gloom and Doom is back.

Anna puts her book down.
Who are those two kids you're hanging out with?

Maggie and Mark,
I tell her.
My new friends.
Their mum's a volunteer.
You should come join us.
They want to meet you.

What about Ella?
What about her?

I can't believe you've already forgotten her?

My hands ball
into tight fists.
Mummy's arms
wrap around
my anger,
holding it
tightly.

My prickly feelings

    Need   Be
         To   Free.

I shove
her away
and run outside.

You Make Me Wanna Shout

I swallow the lump
of tears caught
in my throat
and start running.

Anna is so mean.
It's not my fault
she's stuck inside.
It's not my fault
her lungs don't
like England weather.

She knows
I could never
forget Ella.
She's just jealous
that I've
made two new friends
and she hasn't
met anyone.

I stomp.
My feet sink
into the soggy ground.
I shake my fists
into the air
and sing
at the top
of my lungs,
drowning
out the sting
of Anna's words.

AGHHHHH!
You make me wanna shout!

The Soldier

My singing, dancing body slams straight into
a soldier.

Where're you off to in such a hurry?

The soldier
is tall with skin
the color of molasses.
He looks smarter
and bigger
in his uniform
than the soldiers
in Kampala.
He talks
funny too.
His words
stretching and curving
like a slow-moving river.
He bends down
so his face is close
to mine.

Girl, I heard those lungs.

Then he jumps back
and lifts his arms into the air.

Go on then . . .
SHOUT
Wave your arms up.
SHOUT

I laugh.
He smiles
and his whole face
lights up.

   I'm Leroy.

I'm Viva.

   So Viva, you gonna tell me what has you
   shouting, hollering, raging mad?

I tell him everything.

Ella
~~was~~
is
my best friend.
We're both ten,
have wild, crazy black hair,
and wild, crazy personalities.

We love
the Supremes,
all Motown music,
dancing,
and singing.

Especially singing.

We sing
on our way to school
on our way home
while playing hopscotch
and jumping rope.

I made a pact
with Ella
before she left.

Promise you'll
never stop singing
never stop dancing.

Ella promised.
We shook hands
and did our pinky swear.

Two days later,
she got
on a plane
to Canada
and left
me.

And just like that

another soldier
comes along,
with eyes as blue
as Lake Victoria.
His face is stern
like Mr. D'Souza
when he'd catch
Ella and me
looking through
glossy magazines
instead of doing math.

GET TO WORK, AIRMAN FIRST CLASS!
he bellows.
YOU DON'T GET PAID TO SIT AROUND TALKING TO
LITTLE GIRLS.

Yessir.
My soldier
goes off,
grinning back
at me
over his shoulder.
Then, he's gone too.

Chatting with Mark

Did you know that they're not called soldiers?
  Who?

The men stationed at RAF. They're not called soldiers.
  What are they called?

Airmen, because they do their fighting in the air.
  That makes sense.

Your airman is from America.
  How do you know?

We don't have an Airman First Class rank in the RAF.
  Do they have a different name?

Aircraft man or AC, for short.
  What's your dad?

A Wing Commander.
  He takes care of a wing on the plane?

No. He's in charge of a flying wing.

FLYING WING: a group of three or four aircraft squadrons

(Note to Daddy: Another definition from my living dictionary—Mark.)

Things That Go Bump in the Night

Creaking
Grunting
Snoring
Whispering
Crying
Walking
Rumbling
Praying
Chanting

Thirty of us
squeezed
into this room
in the red brick
barracks.

It

Is

Impossible

To

Sleep!

The Village Grows

Beds are made up
with clean sheets
and blankets.

Clanking
and clamoring
pots and pans
rattle the MESS hall.

Old Mrs. Robinson
is everywhere
screeching orders.

More sweaters
More pants.
Socks and tights.
More Indians are here.
Hurry!

I hurry,
to get right out
of her way.

Nahin

In the three days
we've been here,
I've never seen
the MESS
this full.
So many faces,
in shades
of brown,
squeeze together
on long tables,
but hardly anyone
eats.

Nahin
No!
Mums and Dads
shake their heads
when little hungry fingers
reach for
fat sausages
and crispy bacon.

They ask for
roti and chapati (flatbread)   *Nahin*

dosa (thin crepes made of lentils)   *Nahin*

idlis (steamed rice-dough pancakes)   *Nahin*

Then tears start.
I know
how they feel.
They want something
that reminds them
of home
because . . .
                    Everything here is so DIFFERENT.

33

Locked In

We are free
but not really.
Not if you
count all the
police officers,
smiling
scowling
friendly
frightening
guarding
watching
to make sure
we don't
leave
the designated
Asian area.

Rebel

REBEL: re·bel /'rebəl/
a) to oppose or disobey one in authority or control
b) to act in or show opposition or disobedience

It's what
Mr. D'Souza
used to call me
for always
talking
too much
in class.

It's what
Officer Graham says
when he catches me
crawling through the hole
in the barbed wire
into the American
forbidden zone.

It's what
Anna
calls me
for sneaking
out to watch
planes land
on the airstrip.

I
    am
       the
           rebel.

Hanging Out with Maggie and Mark

I thought you were Indian?
Mark asks.

India has a bunch of different groups,
I tell him and Maggie.

Hindus,
Sikhs,
Bengalis,
Guajaratis,
Punjabis.
Some are vegetarian.
Most don't eat beef.
We speak different languages.
We have different religions.

I'm Goan.
We eat everything.
We speak English, Portuguese, Swahili, and Konkani.
We are Catholic.

Cool.
That's all Mark says.
But I know his brainy brain
is thinking over what I've said.

Tomorrow

Daddy arrives.

6:00 PM
Stansted Airport
United Kingdom

I can't wait!

A Wide Smile

The last time
I saw Daddy,
he hugged me tightly
and told me
to be good and listen
to Mummy.

I noticed
he didn't say
the same thing
to Anna.

Then he
smiled widely
and waved
goodbye.
That was
a week ago.

His smile
has helped ease my
fears,
loneliness,
and worries.

Somehow
it is easier
going to sleep
knowing that
tomorrow
Daddy
will be here.

Knowing
we will
be leaving
this camp
behind and
starting our new life.

A Promise to Maggie

In the morning,
Maggie appears
in the barracks.
She has a surprise
and invites
Anna too.

Anna's busy reading,
I tell her.
Then my sister
announces
she'll come too.

Now, that's a surprise.

Outside,
the cold
pinches
my nose
and cheeks.

Maggie
keeps a steady
downpour
of words
as we hurry
to the common hall.

I can't believe your dad arrives in six hours.
It'll take around two hours to get here from
Stansted Airport,
I figure he'll arrive by 8:30 or 9:00 PM.
I bet you can't wait to see him.
You must be sooooo excited!

40

She pauses,
but I know to keep quiet.
It's Maggie recharging her brain.

I'm really happy for you,
but this means you will be leaving
and I might never see you again
and that will just be terrible.

She says all of this in one breath and then grabs
my arm.

Promise you'll write once you get to Canada.
You have to promise you won't forget me.
It's too awful to imagine never speaking to one
another again. You have to write and tell me
about your new home and what your school is like.
PROMISE.

Anna coughs
and sinks
into her scarf,
but not before
I see her
ever-so-big
eye roll.

I ignore my sister
and give Maggie
a hug full
of promises.

SURPRISE

Ta-dah!
Miss Robinson
stands with
Mark.

A long paper
stretches
across a table.

There are
pots of paint,
crayons,
brushes,
and markers.

Maggie shouts.

    It's to make a welcome sign for your dad.

We get right to it.
Painting.
Drawing.
Writing.

Even Mark,
who likes
things neat
and orderly,
joins in
and writes

WELCOME TO ENGLAND

When we're
all done,
Miss Robinson and Mark
hold it up.

Dad is going to love it. Anna says.
I agree.

Finally, the Bus Arrives

In the distance
a deep rumbling cuts
through the quiet
countryside.
Not the steady
rhythm of the planes
that land
on the long
Greenham runway
but a
grinding,
crunching,
earsplitting,
screech . . .

THE BUS.

The Welcome Committee

We're all here,
bundled
in sweaters
jackets
scarves and gloves.

The wind tugs
and pulls,
but my excitement
keeps the cold out.

For the first time
since arriving
in England,
there is no trace
of worry
or sadness
on Mummy's face.
Her smile is full
of happiness.

Anna and Mark
hold up
the welcome sign.

Maggie,
Mr. and Mrs. Mackay,
and Miss Robinson
wave tiny British flags.

Even grouchy Mrs. Robinson
is here.

A welcome committee for Daddy!

One by one

the passengers
get off
the bus.

I search
every face,
ready
to rush
into Daddy's arms
the second
he gets
off the bus.

    I don't see him.

    I still don't see him.

    The bus is empty.

        Daddy isn't here.

Anna's words
RAM
into
my chest,
knocking
my breath
out.

While Mummy tries

to find out
what's happened,
Anna, Maggie, Mark,
and I think
of reasons why
Daddy isn't here.

He missed his flight.
His plane got delayed.
He flew straight to Canada.
He's at another resettlement camp.
He's sick.
He's in the hospital.
The police detained him.
He was arrested.
He's in Mykende prison.

Then there's that one
horrible,
dreadful,
utterly heartbreaking reason.

The one nobody wants
to say aloud,
but you know
we are all thinking . . .

Daddy is dead.

The last two weeks

ten buses have come from
different airports in England.
I've sneaked out
onto the American side
to wait
at the front gate.

Every time I go,
Anna threatens to tell.
She hasn't.
Yet.
I think it's because
deep down she
wants to come too.
I kind of feel bad
she can't come.
It doesn't
stop
me.

I wait
at the front gate,
shivering
in the cold wind,
drenched
in the steady rain,
but Daddy
doesn't
come.

November 1972

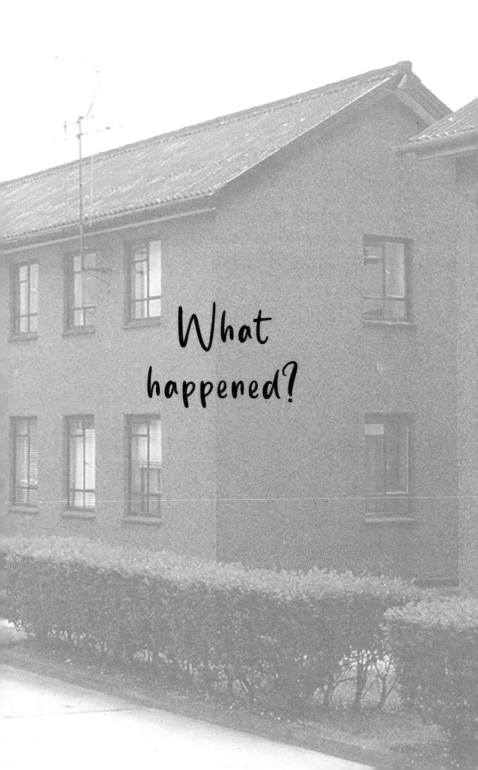

What
happened?

Guy Fawkes

Mark fills us in
as Maggie, Anna, and me
stuff straw inside the scarecrow's shirt.

> *Did you know that Guy Fawkes was part of the*
> *Gunpowder Treason Plot?*
> *Biggest plot in history.*
> *The plan was to blow up Parliament.*
> *Planted bombs right under the king's throne.*
> *On November fifth, when the king sat on the throne,*
> *Guy Fawkes was to set them off.*
> *BOOM!*

What happened?

> *He got caught and was beheaded.*

Maggie jumps in . . .
Every November fifth, we have bonfires
all over England.
Loads of fireworks.
We stuff a dummy and then burn Guy Fawkes.

Sounds awful, Anna says.

Maggie holds up our scarecrow.

I stuff straw deep
into Guy Fawkes's shirt.
It feels good
having something
to look forward to,
something to distract
my worrying head
from thinking
about Daddy.

What a Night!

The whole of RAF is celebrating together.
Americans.
Indians.
British.

The roaring fire keeps the chill away.
Fat sausages sizzle on the end of wooden twigs.
Sticky treacle toffee sticks to my teeth.
Silver sparkles whir round and round.
Bright orange Catherine Wheels spin above the
control tower.
Red Rockets whiz across the fields.
Golden Fountains shower the night sky in brightness.
Guy Fawkes roasts in the fiery flames.

Hip hip hoorah!

Hip hip hoorah!

God save the King!

Mark said that's what the people shouted that night
when they caught Guy Fawkes.
I can't shout.
I'm still licking sticky treacle off my fingers.
Oh, what a night!

Anna won't talk to me.

She's mad because
I've been hanging out
with Maggie and Mark
and she's stuck inside.
It's not my fault
Mummy won't let her outside.
I am going to bust
through her anger wall
and make her talk to me.

A bus is arriving at midnight from Stansted Airport.
I'm going to sneak out again.

Anna keeps reading.
I scoot in right next to her.

I have a good feeling, I tell her. I think Daddy
will be on this one.

Mummy walks over in her pajamas.
*Viva's been going to the American side to wait for
the buses,*
Anna blurts out.
She's sneaking out tonight.

My mouth drops open.
Now I'm the mad one.
I pinch Anna's arm.
    Ow! She elbows my side.

You know we're not allowed on the American side.
You'll get us in trouble, Mummy says.
She tucks me in like a sausage.

52

You are staying here tonight. You are coughing.

Anna grins smugly.

I stick out my tongue at her.
I'm going out tonight.
But I don't say it aloud.
I whisper-sing in my head.

> *I'm going out tonight.*
> *Nothin will keep me,*
> *keep me from you, Daddy.*

Freedom

Mummy and Anna
are finally asleep.
I make my escape,
tiptoeing around
mattresses and cots,
careful not to wake
sleeping heads,
or raise curious glances.

I hold in the coughs
beating at my chest.
I wonder
if Anna's chest
feels like this
all of the time?

I open the door,
dart outside,
and fall against the wall
in a fit of coughs.

The cold air pinches
my lungs, my cheeks, my nose.
I zip my coat,
pull up the hood,
and set off.
It's almost midnight.

I'm free.
Feeling lucky.
I think Daddy
will be on this bus.

Brrrrr

No wind
No rain
Can stop me.

I hunker down
against the windy gusts.
My boots slip
in the soft, wet mud.

Kampala was never
this cold,
this wet,
this windy.
I shiver and cough.
My chest burns.

Shadowy blackbirds
perch on barbed wire fences.
I'm glad for their company.

There's no sign of the bus,
so I wait.
I crouch and pull my knees
to my chest and rock
back and forth
to keep warm.

I shiver. I cough. I wait.

Darkness.

It's Daddy

Smiling

Singing

Shuffling

    Shrinking
        Shrinking
            Shrinking

I wake
shivering,
sweating.

Darkness.

So much darkness.

I'm tired,
      cold,
      alone.

No bus.
No Daddy.

I get up,
   stumble
      and
         fall.

Where am I?

Heaven?
It's . . .
Quiet.
Peaceful.
Warm.

But what's that smell?
Disinfectant!

Heaven should smell
glorious,
like a ripe mango
or sweet papaya.

Footsteps.
It's God.
He's coming over.

My eyes flutter.
Blurred images appear.

God is a woman.
She's wearing a light blue uniform
and white cap.

She says,
You have bronchitis and a mild case of hypothermia.
Close your eyes and sleep.
You're in the infirmary.

A-Hunting We Will Go

Help.
I can't move.
I'm hot.
I'm cold.
My teeth chatter.

I am stuck
in sleep world,
but hearing everything.

All these strange words.
I need Big Blue
Mini Blue
Mark's brain.

Infirmary

Hypothermia

Paracetamol

Anna Visits

Viva,
can you hear me?
You have to wake up.

There's still no news about Daddy.
Mrs. Robinson took Mummy to the post office and
she sent telegrams to Kampala.

Mummy is so worried and blames herself for you
getting sick.

I told her that there's just no stopping you, but
she's still blaming herself.

Wake up!
Viva.

If you don't wake up, I'm going to read *The House
At Pooh Corner* and then I won't stop until I've
read every single Pooh book and you know that
little bear drives you crazy.

Viva?

I'm sorry I was crabby to you the other night.
Please wake up.
You've been asleep for two days.
Wake up.
I miss my sister.

And, I know you like having your wordbook with you,
so I put it in the drawer.

Maggie Visits

Oh Viva, I've been sooooo worried about you.
I can't believe you were out in the cold.
Your mum says you'll be fine.
Your body is resting so it can recover, and when it's
done, you'll wake up.
Please hurry.
      I am SOOOOO bored without you.
It's our half-term break so I'm volunteering at the
camp with Mummy.
Oh, I met your American Airman.
He is dishy.
Those dark eyes.
His bright smile.
I hardly understand a word he says, but I don't care.
I love listening to him talk in his Yankee accent.
Did you know that he rescued you?
He was on patrol with another airman and they saw you.
He picked you up and brought you here.
If it wasn't for him, who knows what
would have happened.
He is your knight in shining armor.
Well not armor, more like army greens.
I could stare at him all day.
And you could too, if you'd only hurry and wake up.

Oh no!
Sister Crotchety Carol is back and she's
making eyes at me.
There's one good thing about you being asleep.
You don't have to talk to her.
She is a scary nurse and she's coming this way.
Got to go.

Hurry and wake up.

Mummy Visits

Get better, my darling girl.
Rest.
You have to be strong to sing to your father when
he gets here.
I'm off to the post office.
Mrs. Robinson said a telegram is waiting for me.
I'm hoping it's news about your father.
Sister Carol is taking good care of you.

Mark Visits

Hello Viva.
I had to wait
for Sister Crotchety to leave
so I could sneak in.

Did you know that
you're in a sleep state
because of the hypothermia?
Your body temperature
is back to normal,
37°C,
but it must have
dropped below
35°C.

You look the same,
like any minute
you'll sit up
and start singing.
I'll stop staring now
because it is
kind of creepy
and I don't want
to be here
when Sister Crotchety
gets back.

I have a gift for you.
I'm putting it
inside the drawer
of your side table.

Hurry and wake up.
Maggie is driving me nuts.

Bye.

Awake

It's the middle
of the night
and I'm wide-awake.

Sister Carol
did all the nurse things.
Took my temperature.
Counted my pulse.
Listened to my heart.
And made me
take deep breaths.

You'll be out of here this afternoon, she says.
Afternoon can't come
soon enough
for me.

Mark's Gift: A Note

Hello Viva,
Here's something I think you will like. WORDS
and DEFINITIONS to add to your wordbook.

INFIRMARY: in·fir·ma·ry /in'fərm(ə)rē/
a place for the care of those who are ill, like a hospital

HYPOTHERMIA: hy·po·ther·mi·a /ˌhīpə'THərmēə/
the condition of having an abnormally low body
temperature, typically one that is dangerously low

I looked them up for you.
Mark

There's More On The Back

P.S. Hi Viva.
It's Maggie. I found Mark's note and it is so
BORING.

You need something fun.

Here's my word:

CANTANKEROUS: can·tan·ker·ous /kan'taNGk(ə)rəs/
bad-tempered, argumentative, and uncooperative

I think this is the perfect word to describe
someone in a light blue uniform and white cap.
Hmmmm, who do you think that is?

Hurry and wake up.
Oh wait.
Silly me.
If you are reading this note you are awake.

XOXO Maggie

Sister Cantankerous Carol is back.

I'm starving. Did you bring me some fish and chips?
It's Bovril and toast for you, Sister Carol says.
The kitchen is closed. It's the middle of the night.

What's Bovril?
It's beef broth.

This smells funny. Can't I have kunji and a chapati?
What is that?

Kunji is boiled rice soup.
Chapati is like bread, but it's flat and fried.
Slathered in butter . . . Yum!
You will just have to pretend the broth is Kungeeli
and your toast is a chap.

Kunji and chapati!
You should get a wordbook, like mine, to help you
remember new words.

That's enough from you, Missy.
Now, drink your broth.

Sadness Seeps In

It is taking forever
for morning to appear.
I add Mark's words
to my book
and watch the shadows
outside the window change.

Blobs turn into
trees,
bushes,
jeeps,
people.

Raindrops run
down the window
like long tears.

I heard lots
of voices
when I was
in my deep sleep,
but not the one I wanted.
DADDY.

I clutch my wordbook
against my heart.
It makes me
feel closer to him.

Surprise Visitor

Well, if it isn't Sleeping Beauty.
About time you woke up.

Howdy, Leroy.

Howdy right back at you, Lil' Diana Ross.

What are you doing up? It's the middle of the night.

I just finished unloading mail from an aircraft that
got in late.
I'm heading to the barracks to get some sleep and
thought I'd see how you're doing.
Looks like you'll be back to singing any day now.

I heard you found me.
Asante sana.

Asante, what?

Asante sana.
It's thank you very much in Swahili.

Daddy Update

1. Daddy checked into the Entebbe Airport

2. He never got on the plane

3. Nobody has seen him

4. Nobody knows where he is

Anna Has News

While you were sleeping . . .

I wasn't sleeping. I was sick.

Listen. This is important.
We have to leave RAF camp.

What? Why?

Something about this place being temporary.

Where are we supposed to go?

They have people figuring out that stuff.
Finding us a town and a place to live . . .

Did Mummy tell them that we're only staying at
the base until Daddy comes
and then we're going to Canada?

She tried, but . . .

Good. Then we're staying.

I think the hypothermia affected your hearing.
THE DIRECTOR TOLD MUMMY THAT WE HAVE TO LEAVE.

You don't have to shout! I heard you the first time.

Where Is Southall?

Mrs. Robinson told Mummy that we
are going to be settled in Southall.

I look up Southall in the *A-Z Atlas and Guide to London.*
It's in the west part of London
in a borough.
Miss Robinson tells me
that borough is another word
for town.

I'd like
to burrow
and hide
from my life.

Southall is in the Borough of Ealing.
Sixty miles from Greenham Common.
That's like making three trips
from Kampala to Entebbe.

Sixty miles
is a LONG way
when you don't know the country.

How will Daddy find us?

While Mummy meets

with people
about our move
to Southall
Anna and I go
to the library
to ease our missing and loneliness.
Anna picks out books.
I look up words
in Mini Blue.
Miss Robinson hums
and organizes the shelves.
Mrs. Robinson sets out
the daily newspapers.

The Telegraph
The Daily Mail
The Guardian
The Times

This isn't good, she says.
I glance up
from Mini Blue
and a chill runs
                    down
                        my
                            spine.

HEADLINES

I can't stop staring
at the fat, black letters
stamped across the front page
of every newspaper.

NO MORE ASIANS

Why Do I Bother?

Anna, did you see this?   *No.*

Stop reading and look!   *No more Asians.*

It says Southall.
SOUTHALL   *AND?*

We are going there and
they don't want us.   *Nobody wants us, Viva.*
                         Not President Amin.
                         Not those people at Southall.
                         Not the people here at the camp.
                         N-O-B-O-D-Y
                         NOBODY!

What's wrong with you?
                         Wake up, Viva!
                         This is our life.
                         No Kampala.
                         No Canada.
                         No Daddy.
                         Now, leave me alone!

Anna clutches her books to her chest and STORMS out.
I hate you!
I shout after her.

SHHH!

If you cannot use a quiet voice, you will have to leave.
Mrs. Robinson
points her red tipped finger
        at me.

73

Escape

I heard you and Anna, Miss Robinson says.

When I don't answer,
she points to the newspaper.

Was it about this?

Anna is so mean,
I tell her.
She doesn't care about anything except her books.

I think she cares a lot, and books are her way to escape.

I think about this
as I walk back
to the barracks.

RAF Greenham

is bursting,
too full with Indians.

I used to have space
to sing
to dance
to breathe.

Wherever Daddy is,
he needs to get to England
and save me.
FAST!

I am suffocating.

In with the new

and out with the old.

My head is spinning
at how fast
they are moving Indians out
of RAF Greenham camp
into towns and villages.

Mrs. Robinson
and the round, red-faced director
talk
plan
whisper.

We are next.
I know it!
Those angry faces
from the newspaper
haunt my dreams
and shout in my head.

NO MORE ASIANS.

Prayer

Different shades
of brown.
Different beliefs.

Hinduism
Islam
Sikhism
Buddhism
Jainism
Christianity . . . Me, Mummy, and Anna.

But
we all have
the same prayer.
Please,
please,
please.
Make everything all right.

Chatting with Officer Graham

What are you doing up in the oak, Viva?
Praying.

Is this where Hindus pray?
I don't know. I'm Catholic.

*The chapel is just down the hill and probably safer
than up in a tree.*
I figured God would hear me better with no roof
between us.
Just open sky.

*We have the same God, and he can hear you just as
well down here.*
Daddy always says, two is better than one.
Will you pray with me if I come down?

What are we praying for?
For God to keep Daddy safe and bring him to
England so I don't have to go to Southall.

God must be deaf,

I tell Anna.
I've prayed
every day
since I learned
we have to
leave the base
and still there's
no word
about Daddy.

NOTHING

I've prayed
to Saint Anthony,
the patron saint
of lost things,
asking him
to find Daddy,
bring him here
so we can go
to Canada.
NOT
Southall.

That's how
desperate
I
am.

STILL NOTHING

The runway

is the one place

    I can breathe.

The wind rolls
down the long
concrete runway
and grabs me
in its gusty arms
and my lungs
fill with air.

I feel
safe here
and don't want
to leave
but nobody
cares what
I want.

All I hear is . . .

It's time for you to go!

Marmite and Marmalade Picnic

Maggie and Mark show up
with a basket of goodies.
Bread.
Marmite.
Scones.
Marmalade.
Hot tea.

The Marmite spread,
thick and gooey,
smells
as bad as it looks,
and tastes
even worse.
I miss Cook's
green chutney sandwiches.

But I'll eat
the entire pot
of Marmite
if it means
I could freeze time,
here, right now
with Maggie and Mark
and never have
to leave RAF Greenham.

But that's
not happening
so I reach
for a scone
instead.

You can't go there!

Mark says
when I tell him
and Maggie
that we're going
to Southall.

Mr. Gupta lives there.
I tell them.
Daddy worked with
his brother
in Kampala.

We're going
to stay
with his family
until Daddy
arrives.

Mark shakes his head.
But
Southall
is
RED!

Red Zone Areas

Southall
Leicester
Bradford
Have too many Asians.
They don't want any more.
Especially Southall!

    Stop talking, Mark, Maggie says.

My head spins.
A tsunami
grows inside me
ready to explode.

Mark ignores Maggie and continues.
I hear . . .

Protests.
Picketers.
No More Asians.
Want the government to send you back.
Too many colored people.
No more refugees.

    Shut up! Maggie shoves Mark.

The tsunami
engulfs me.
I can't breathe
and scramble
to escape.

    VIVA! COME BACK.

I don't stop.
I keep running
from all the fears
chasing me.

I rush

past airmen
unloading mail sacks,
past noisy planes,
blurring in the distance,
past Officer Graham
coming out of the MESS,
past men
holding wobbly turbans,
and women
clutching flying dupatta scarves.

I run
to escape
this life
waiting
with its
grubby, grabby claws.

The wind is a growling monster

attacking me from all sides,
pushing
pulling
grasping.

A tall brick tower
stands ahead.
I rush
around
the backside
and sink
to the ground.

SILENCE

Chatting with Leroy

Whatcha doing out by the control tower, Lil' Diana?
I want to go home to Kampala.

Don't think it's this way.
I don't want to, but I can't help it.
Leroy makes me smile.

That's what I like to see. What's up?
I hate it here. Well, not here on the base, but out there.

How do you know what it's like if you haven't been there?
People have signs: No More Asians.
They don't want me, Leroy.

*Don't let that stop you from going where you want to go
and doing what you want to do.*
That's just it. I don't want to go there.

But if you did, you could show them a thing or two.
You don't get it.

I get it more than you think, Lil' Diana.

Leroy's Story

My mom's white.
My dad's black.
I'm a little bit of both—brown.
White kids made fun of me for being black.
Black kids made fun of me for not being black
enough.

I'd crawl under my bed and hide.
But Mamma wouldn't have it.
No way!
She'd drag me out by my feet and say,
No boy of hers was going to hide from life.

She told me . . .

> You get courage
> by doing small things,
> one at a time.

If you're anything like
Diana Ross,
which I think
you are,
then there's
a whole lot
of courage
inside you, Lil' Diana
and it's just
waiting
to come out
a little bit
at a time.

I find a bit of courage

to bring back Diana
in all of her Supremeness
and Leroy and me sing
all the way
back
to the barracks.

One Last Try

Why do we have to leave?
I challenge Mummy
to tell me the truth.

The silence between us
is endless.
Her round, dark eyes
fill with tears
which makes my heart hurt.

Anna scowls at me. *Leave her alone.*

Mummy holds out her hands
to Anna and me.
She says Daddy's supervisor
was arrested by
President Amin's soldiers.
She says nobody
can give her information
about Daddy.

He's not coming, is he?
Anna whispers.
Mummy squeezes
our hands tighter.
She tells us that
we have to go on
with our lives.
It's what Daddy
would have wanted.

I can't believe you're giving up, I shout.
I stomp outside,
my whole body
shakes and trembles.

I shiver against

the wind
stinging my nose
and cheeks,
wishing I'd stopped
for my coat.

Stars are sown
across the night sky.
Daddy told me
that behind each star
wishes and dreams hide.

I'm not giving up
on Daddy
like Mummy and Anna.
I refuse.

I stare at the furthest star
and wonder
if Daddy sees the same star.
If the same wish,
to see one another again,
hides behind
that star.

The Farthest Star

I don't see
Officer Graham
until he sits
on the grass
beside me.

What are you doing? he asks.

I point
to the farthest star
and tell him
that I wish
Daddy was here.

He doesn't say
everything will be okay,
or it will all work out,
which makes me think
he understands.

An idea sparks
and I know
that this
is my one chance.
Tomorrow will be
too late.

I look up
at that farthest star
and dig deep
for the courage
to take that
one small
step.

A Promise

I take a deep breath,
filling my lungs
with courage.
Will you help me find out what's happened to my father?
His name is Charlie DaSilva.

SILENCE.
I worry Officer Graham didn't hear me.
But then . . .

I will try, Viva.

Thank you!
I grab his hand.
Promise.

I promise to try, but I can't promise I'll get answers.

As we walk back
to the barracks,
I can't help thinking
how Officer Graham looks
a little like Father Christmas,
without the big belly,
a brown beard instead
of a white one.
Still, Father Christmas.

Maybe it's because
his promise
is like a
gift.

Gift from Leroy

I got you something.

What is it? I ask Leroy.

Open it.

 WINGS

You're a spunky bird, Lil' Diana.
When you're down because of your troubles,
and you want to fold up your wings,

DON'T do it.

Spread those wings wide

Soar

high above the skies of gray,

Higher

than the storms gathering.

Face life's storms, Viva.

Be STRONG.

Be COURAGEOUS.

SOAR!

My Last Night at RAF Greenham Base

I can't sleep
with all the noise
in my head.
My heart races
thinking
about the picketers
waiting for us
in Southall.

Fear

Daddy
would want me
to be courageous,
like the time
I went swimming
in the sea
with waves so big
I thought they'd
swallow me whole.
He was right there
beside me
when I dived in.

I look at my wings.

How do I soar above my fears?

How?
When Daddy
isn't here
beside
me.

We've got to go.
Anna stands in front of me,
her Enid Blyton book
tucked under her arm.
She holds out her hand.
I take it.
She squeezes my fingers.
It will be okay,
Anna says softly
and we walk out,
hand in hand,
together.

Packed and Ready to Go

Before I get
out of the jeep
I hear them
singing . . .

> Listen Viva.
> This one's for you . . .

Everyone's
come to say goodbye.
Miss Robinson,
Leroy,
Officer Graham,
Maggie,
Mark,
Old Mrs. Robinson,
and even Sister Crotchety Carol.

My own Supremes Chorus.

> Don't worry, Viva.
> If you need us.
> Call!
> And we'll hurry over.

I wave
and shout goodbyes.
With wet eyes
and a choked voice,
I climb into Mr. Gupta's car.

Goodbye . . .

crowded barracks
with
snoring,
farting,
whispering,
crying strangers.

MESS
with soupy dal,
tasteless curry,
and scrummy fish and chips.

Common Room
with Mini Blue,
Old Mrs. Robinson,
cinema nights,
and sparkly Miss Robinson.

Suffocating feelings
and no room
to breathe.

Goodbye . . .
safe camp.
Protected.
Secure.
Friendly.

Goodbye friends.
Leroy,
Officer Graham,
Maggie and Mark.

Goodbye RAF Greenham Common.

December 1972

Britons Unite with the National Front

Why didn't you tell us?

The Drive

Outside
the window,
sky,
fields,
buildings,
blur.

Mr. Gupta
speeds
along the motorway,
taking us
deep
into the web
of twisted streets,
narrow alleyways,
deep
into the web of London.

I wonder
what big fat spider
waits for us
in the middle
of its web.

An angry mob.

Scowling picketers.

HATE.

Uncle and Auntie

My brother speaks well about your father,
Mr. Gupta tells Anna and me.

Thank you, Mr. Gupta,
I say.

None of this formality.
Call us Varun Uncle and Meena Auntie.

I smile and nod.
It's like that
with Indians.
All grown-ups
are uncle or auntie.

Questions

Is your brother still in Kampala?
 Did you talk to him?
  Does he know what happened to Daddy?
   Has he seen Daddy at the office?
    Does anybody know anything about my dad?

Round and round,
questions spin,
so fast
my head feels like
it's going to burst
and there is only
one way
to make it stop.
I ask Varun Uncle.

I told your mother everything I know, he says.
Mr. Stewart, your father's boss, made some
disparaging comments about senior African politicians.

Note to self:
Look up **disparaging**
and add to wordbook.

Your father went to the British High Commission in
Kampala to inquire about Mr. Stewart when he didn't
show up at the office.

I look at Anna.
She keeps her face hidden behind her book,
but she hasn't turned the page in a while.
I know she's listening.

What does that have to do with him being missing?
I ask.

*The authorities suspect your father of being a spy
for the British.*

Anna drops her book and looks right at me.

That's **preposterous** (another one of Daddy
and my favorite words).

A spy.
Daddy?
Impossible.
The sides
of his mouth
curl upward
whenever he tries
to trick us.
I remember when he
brought home Chickoo.
He tried
to tell
Anna and me
we couldn't have
a dog
and giggled
the whole time
the tiny dachshund
squirmed inside his jacket.

More I Didn't Know

Like I told your mother,
Varun Uncle continues,
best thing you can do, is to carry on.
We will help you get settled
into your new life,
here.

What the Heck?

I can't
believe
that all this time
Mummy knew
this stuff
about Daddy
and didn't
tell me.

And what's this stuff
about settling?
There's no settling.
Not here.
Not without Daddy.

Anna senses my anger
and puts her hand
on mine,
like that will stop me.

It doesn't.

My anger
cracks like thunder
and explodes
filling all the space
inside Varun Uncle's tiny beetle bug car.

Downpour

How long have you known about Daddy?
We'll talk about it later, Viva.

Why didn't you tell us?
I push.

Shhhhh!
Anna squeezes my fingers.

Mummy stays silent.
Her lips tighten
and I know she
is holding in her words
because of Varun Uncle.
It makes me push
harder.

I can't believe you lied.
Daddy wouldn't have lied.

Varun Uncle clears his throat.
Viva, your mummy is doing her best.

But . . .
I start to say.

Mummy cuts me off.
I said we will talk about this later.

I told you to keep quiet,
Anna says.
I pull my hand
out of her too-tight,
know-it-all
grip.

Southall

Varun Uncle lives
on a narrow street
with two long rows
of red brick houses
squished together.
House after house.
Door after door.
The same.

The door opens
and a woman
in a green sari
steps outside.
A boy follows.
He's fair skinned
like his mother
and has Varun Uncle's
plump cheeks
and curly black hair,
but it's his shifty eyes
that I don't trust.

I can tell
we won't be friends.

Why do they have to stay in my room?

Sanjeev asks again,
still glaring at Anna and me
with his buggy, shifty eyes.
I knew I was right about him.

We talked about this,
Varun Uncle says.
It has bunk beds and room for a cot.

Sanjeev trudges upstairs
to his bedroom
muttering,
and we follow
on reluctant feet.

The geometric wallpaper
makes me dizzy,
and the smell
of a thousand farts
is everywhere.

Don't touch anything!
Sanjeev snarls.

As if?

I wouldn't touch anything
if he begged me.
I don't want to be here,
in Southall,
in this house,
in this room.
But I have no choice.
I have no voice.

What I want doesn't matter.

That Night

The aroma of
fragrant basmati rice,
nutty cooked lentils,
sizzling onion and garlic
curls up the stairs,
under the door,
drifting
to the top bunk bed.
It reminds me
of home.
Cook's chicken xacuti
was my favorite.
He always added
just the right amount
of grated coconut.

*Remember that the Guptas have invited us into
their home,*
Mummy says to Anna and me.
Let's have a nice supper.
No matata.

Matata
is Swahili
for trouble.
It's a warning
from Mummy
to Anna and me
to behave
but she's looking
right at me.

Not both of us.

So unfair.

More Naan Please

The best way
to stop
from saying
something
wrong
is to keep
my mouth full.

Full of
chewy naan,
turmeric cauliflower,
and spicy dal
so there's
absolutely no way
      my words
            can slip
                  out
                        of
                              my
                                    mouth.

Table Chattering

We can go shopping on the High Street,
Meena Auntie says.

Another piece
of naan right
into my mouth.

Nope!
Don't need new clothes.

Meet new friends
Nope!

Chatter swirls
around me.
I keep my head down
and my mouth full.

Find you a church
Get you settled
Learn to get around
Nope,
Nope,
Nope!

Tomorrow we will get the girls registered for school.
There is a long waiting list because of all the Indians
moving here.
Nope.

WAIT. WHAT?

This Isn't Happening

I stare at Mummy.
She doesn't look surprised.
Did she know about this?
I kick Anna.
She shakes her head
and gives me her best
mummy-warning look.

Am I
the only one
that remembers
we aren't supposed
to be staying
in London?

What is wrong
with them?
It's like
they've given up
on Daddy
and the life
we'd planned.

Well, not me!
I hear Diana singing
to me about being
shook out
of your world.

Mummy dragged me
to Southall,
but there is no way
I'm going
to school here.

No School for Me

I don't want them at my school.
Sanjeev coughs the words, choking on his rice
and lentils.

Don't worry,
I shoot back.
We don't want to be there!

Viva.
Mummy's voice tells me to let this go.
I can't.

I'm not going to school here.
I can wait until we get to Canada.
I challenge Mummy.

Now isn't the time for this discussion.
Mummy is wearing her I-mean-business voice.

I look to Anna for backup, but she's staring at her
plate like it's the crown jewels.
I'm not going and you can't make me,
I say louder this time.

Awesome!
Sanjeev smiles smugly and snatches the last piece
of jalebi before I can grab it.

Ugh!

Wait for it . . .

Any minute
Mummy will erupt.
Lesson one
that all
Indian kids learn
is you never
embarrass
your parents
in front
of other Indian parents.

Which is exactly
what I've done
in front
of the Gupta family.
Not once.
But twice.

I wait for the scolding.

Nothing.

Mummy walks us
upstairs,
tells us
to get ready
for bed,
and walks out.

Anna finally decides to talk.

You shouldn't have said anything,
Anna says from the bottom bunk.

I peer down from above.
You should have said something.

Anna sits up and looks right at me.
This isn't easy for Mummy.
Living here with strangers.
Alone with the two of us.
You should be nicer to her.
She's missing Daddy, too.

This is the most I've heard Anna say since we
arrived in London.
Okay, maybe that's a bit of an exaggeration.
(Another favorite from my wordbook)
I do feel kind of bad.
But not enough to go to school with Sanjeev.

Guilt

Footsteps
creak
outside the door.

Mummy enters
with two steaming mugs
of turmeric milk.
Her eyes,
wet and shiny,
betray her hurt.

This isn't easy for Mummy.
Anna's words drum in my head.

Guilt
squeezes
my insides.

I'm sorry,
I whisper.

Mummy sighs.
We taught you to act properly in public.
We taught you when to bite your words.

Tears slide
down my cheek.
It's not fair.
You should be finding Daddy.
Not getting settled here.
Not making me go to school.

I take a big gulp,
swallowing the milk
with my words
to stop them
from flying out
of my mouth.

Mummy is blind

to Meena Auntie's
shenanigans.

The extra
gulab jamun,
samosas,
and roti
only for Sanjeev.

The pretending
she forgot
to leave
us a key
so we had to
stand outside
in the rain,
waiting.

NOT ME!

I'm onto her.
Watch out
Meanie Auntie.
Viva has a plan.

> **SHENANIGANS: she·nan·i·gans /SHə'nanəgənz/**
> silly or high-spirited behavior; mischief

My Plan

1. Pretend to be sick so I can skip school shopping.

2. Phone Daddy's office in Uganda.

3. Phone Maggie about returning to RAF Greenham.

4. Surprise Mummy and Anna with the good news when they return from shopping.

5. Leave Southall and Sanjeev's fart-smelling room to move in with Maggie.

Wow,
Look at me.
I'm doing fabulously.

She's back.
I channel
my inner
Supremeness.

Anna Bursts In

Meena Auntie
said
to tell you
to stop singing.
You're giving
her a headache.

Bet nobody
told Diana Ross
to stop singing.
I throw
the covers
over my head
and sing
into my pillow.

Too Many

How can you have
too many brown kids
in one class?

We had nearly
all brown kids
at my school in Kampala.

Here they have a number.
Only two or three per class.
Then you go on a waiting list.
Anna and me are on the list.

I don't care.
I say,
good thing the schools
in Southall
are too full up with Indians.
It gives me a little time
to work on my plan.

I don't care if I stay on the LIST forever!

For my plan

to work,
I need everyone out
of the house.
I tried using the phone
yesterday when it was only
Mummy, Anna, and me
at home, but Mummy
caught me.
I told her
I heard the phone ringing.
Her eyes narrowed
and her Mummy lie radar
clicked on.
She knows
I'm up to something.

Running Out of Time

How did this happen?
We
start
school
in four days.
Me in Year 6.
Anna in Year 7.

Aaghhhhh!

What am I going to do?

I wish
Ella
was here.
Whenever
we have
a problem
we call
an emergency
WWDD
meeting.

What Would Diana Do?

It's hard
to hold a meeting
with only one person.
Me.
And there is no way
I can trust Anna.
What if she blabs
to Mummy?

Christmas

If life isn't bad enough.
Now this!
The Guptas are Hindus.
They don't celebrate Christmas.
That means . . .
Neither will we.
No tree.
No decorations.
No gifts.
No Christmas carols.
No Daddy dressed up as Father Christmas.

NO CHRISTMAS!

Boxing Day

I feel
a tummy ache
coming on.
Meanie Auntie is taking
us shopping
to buy school uniforms
and supplies.
There are big sales today.

Boxing Day.

It's a weird name
for the day after Christmas,
but if it means that the house
will be empty,
then I don't care what they call it.
Varun Uncle and Sanjeev
will be out too.
Soccer practice.

It's the perfect day
to put my plan into action.

Plan Part 1: Pretend to Be Sick

Oww!
I groan to Mummy.
I don't feel well.

COLLYWOBBLES: col·ly·wob·bles /ˈkälēˌwäbəlz/
stomach pain or queasiness

Success!
The door clicks.
I count to ten,
just to be sure,
then tear down the stairs.

Plan Part 2: Phone Uganda

The telephone directory
is thick, filled with many pages.
Uganda's country code
is 256.

I lift the handset, listening
to the dial tone
drone
in my ear.

My tummy
has the collywobbles
for real now.

> **COLLYWOBBLES: col·ly·wob·bles /ˈkälēˌwäbəlz/**
> stomach pain or queasiness
> Intense anxiety or nervousness

Long distance calls
cost a lot of money.
Mummy
will be furious
if she finds out,
but I can't
let that stop me.

I take a deep breath.
Rub my wings for good luck.
One small step at a time.
That's what Leroy told me.

I dial O.
Operator.
I'd like to make a long distance call to Uganda.

Conversation

Hello. May I speak to Mr. DaSilva?

Sorry, he isn't here.

Do you know when he'll be back?

He's not coming back.

When was he last in?

He hasn't been here for a few weeks.

Do you know where he is?

London. He was meeting his family.

But I'm his family and he didn't arrive in London.

I'm sorry. I cannot help you.

Please. There must be something
you can tell me. Anything.

Hello?

Hello?

This is NOT how this conversation was supposed
to go!

Plan Part 3: Phone Maggie

The phone
rings and rings.
Come on, Maggie,
pick up.
Finally . . .

Hello.
Um hello, Mrs. Mackay. It's Viva. Is Maggie home?

Viva?
Yes. I really need to talk—

*Oh, Viva. Maggie really misses you. She was just
saying the other day how going to the base to
volunteer isn't nearly as much fun as it was when
you were there.*

Maggie's mum
is just like her.
A non-stop talker.
I try again.

I really need Maggie's help—

Oh, No!

Who is Maggie?
Startled,
I drop the phone
and spin around.
Sanjeev.
He's supposed to be
at soccer practice.

What are you doing here?
I ask.

He looks
at the phone
on the ground
and cord
in my hand.

I forgot my cleats.
What are you doing?

I wasn't feeling well.
I pick up the phone.

Who's Maggie?
he asks again.

My mind spins
to find an answer.
If Sanjeev blabs,
and I know he will,
I'll be in all kinds
of trouble.
But right now,
I can't think about that.
I have to think
of what I can say
to shut him up.

Sounds

Key rattling
Door squeaking
Footsteps creaking
Voices laughing
Bags rustling

Then,
Mummy . . .
Viva, we're back!

All eyes are on me.

The silence
grows,
stretching
to fill the space
in the room.

The weight
of the phone,
still in my hand,
is heavy
with guilt.

CAUGHT!

Blabbermouth

Viva rang some Maggie person,
Sanjeev says.
He's such a blabbermouth.
I didn't even get a chance to defend myself.
   Shut up!

And that's not all.

My heart jumps.
I throw the phone book,
but he ducks
and it hits the ground.

She asked the operator to call Kampala.

Mummy and Meanie Auntie
GASP.

I glare at Sanjeev with my best stink eye.

   TATTLETALE!
   Stay out of my business.

It's too late.
Mummy knows he's telling the truth.
I'm sent to my room,
which is technically
Sanjeev's room.

Agghhhhhh!
I hate my life.

News!

As I stomp upstairs,
Meanie Auntie says something
that makes me freeze.

She tells Mummy . . .

Nehal said you can move in on Friday.
You'll have the weekend to settle into the flat
before the girls start school
and you start your job.

A Home of Our Own

Meena Auntie
has a friend
who owns a building
of small flats.
He's renting one
to Mummy
and we are moving out.

Finally,
I can get away
from Sanjeev
and his stinky room.

Bags and more bags

from the
High Street.
Sheets,
towels,
pans,
plates,
cups,
cutlery,
blankets,
pillows
are stacked
wide and tall
like a tower.

Things
for the
new home.

I worry Mummy
is getting
too settled in London.
Too settled
in this new life
without
Daddy.

January 1973

This

is

no

house.

Our new house

is only
one bus stop away
from the Guptas' house
on another
long street
with rows upon rows
of houses.

I wonder
which one
is ours.

This is no house.

It's one floor,
a narrow corridor,
one tiny bedroom,
a window
that barely
lets in any
light,
a too-small
kitchen
with wobbly
chairs,
wallpaper
the color of dried dal,
and a muddy brown sofa.
It's the ugliest thing
I've ever seen.

Lies

What do you think?

Meanie Auntie jumps in
to fill the uncomfortable silence.

*Um . . . I know it's not what you're used to, but
it's very nice. Yes?*

Thank you. It will be fine,
Mummy says.
She tries to smile,
but it is an effort.

Mummy can make any place look good,
Anna says.

I glare at Anna
until her fake smile slips.
Not even Mummy
can turn this place around.

It's a dump.
Meanie Auntie
would never ever
in a million years
stay in this place.
And that's exactly
what I tell her.
The truth!

If you like it so much, you should stay here.

I don't know,

I tell Mummy
when she asks
why I say these things.

I don't know
why the mean thoughts
in my head fly out
of my mouth.

I don't know
why I feel
angry,
sad,
and lonely
all the time.

I don't know
why my life
turned horribly
wrong.

I do know
that I miss
everything
about my old life,
the sun,
friendly faces,
Ella,
and most
especially
Daddy.

Supper

Familiar smells
drift through the small flat.
Fragrant tendrils of
earthy cumin,
pungent coriander,
aromatic turmeric.
Reminders of home.
Kampala.
So much has changed
in the last few weeks,
but Mummy's cooking
is the same.

In the too-small kitchen,
we squeeze
around the table
for our first supper together.

Mummy prays.
God, thank you for this food.

Then she scoops
spoonfuls of lamb biryani
onto each of our plates.
I breathe in the
spicy deliciousness
and my mouth waters.
The Guptas only
served vegetarian dishes.
I can't wait to eat the
fluffy grains of rice
and marinated pieces of lamb.

Mummy holds
our hands.

Wait a minute, she says.

The sadness
in her voice
makes my eyes
prickle.
She clears her throat
and I know
she's going
to say something
about Daddy.
She squeezes
our fingers
and says . . .

Rub-a-dub-dub
Let's dig in to this grub.

I can't believe it!
This is what Daddy
always says
before we eat,
right after we thank God
for our food.

Anna looks at me.
We both look at Mummy.
Then we all start laughing.
We laugh and laugh
until our eyes tear.
It's been
a long time
since I've heard
our laughter.
It sounds the same.
It's good to know
that's one thing
that hasn't
changed.

Night Prayers

God,
thank you
for saving me
from spending
another night
in Sanjeev's stinky fart bedroom.

I don't think that's how you are supposed to pray,
Anna says and takes over.
Dear God,
Thank you for keeping us safe and . . .

While Anna prays
I wonder if God
has stopped listening
to my prayers because
of the things I've done . . .
Talking back to Meanie Auntie.
Lying to Mummy.
Phoning Uganda without permission.
Then I get nervous.
What if that's the reason Daddy hasn't come?
God is mad at me.
Before I climb into
bed with Anna
I add an extra prayer.
I keep it between
God and me.

Dear God,
I promise to do better.
No more lies and I'll use kind words.
Listen to Mummy.
Oh, and this is Viva, in case you don't know.

Spring Term Starts

The school
is a five-minute walk
from the flat.
Mummy timed it
when she showed us
the way yesterday
and made us
promise to stay together.
Worries
tug and tie
my tummy in knots.
Thoughts
race in my head.

    I hate this school.
    I don't want any part of it.
    I'm not going.
    Please don't make me go.

    Shhhh!
    Shut-up, Viva.

I remember my
promise to God,
and push down
my angry words.

Dreaded thoughts

line up
in my head . . .

Will I like my new teachers?

What will my classmates be like?

Will they pick on me?

Will they make fun of me?

Will I make any friends?

What if nobody likes me?

What if I don't know anything?

First Day of School

I was less afraid
of getting off the bus
at RAF Greenham
when we first
arrived in England
than I am of what's
waiting for me.

Anna and I
stay together
until we step through
the double doors
into this strange,
disinfectant-smelling
new world.
I'll meet you right here by the water fountain,
Anna says, disappearing
and leaving me.

I slip my hand
inside my pocket
and squeeze my wings,
digging for a bit of courage.

Here I go.
My head held high,
walking down the corridor.
Kids rush past me
from every direction.
I know from the way
they don't meet my eyes
that I am not welcome.
My shoulders droop,
wilting like a daisy
in the too-hot afternoon sun.

Just AWFUL

My first day was horrible,
I tell Mummy.
My teacher hates me.
The math is too hard.
I did the wrong page in English.
The kids are mean, even the Indian ones.
They think I'm stupid.
And you haven't even heard the worst yet.

Mrs. Wright,
my new teacher,
decided it would
be good
if the new Indian girl
sat with the only
other Indian kid
in class.
So I am stuck
sitting in the back
with a boy.

And not any boy . . .

SANJEEV!

Did you hear me, Mummy?

SANJEEV!

Daddy Update

There's been
no news
about Daddy.
No phone calls.
No telegrams.
No letters.
I ask Mummy every day.
Every day it's the same answer.

I don't know anything more than what I knew yesterday.
When I find out something, I'll tell you girls.

But that's the problem.
I don't know if Mummy
is trying to find out something.

Grunwick

Mummy started her new job.
She does something
with camera film
and photos
and comes home smelling
of chemicals.
I miss Kampala Mummy
who smelled
of warm sandalwood
and sweet rosewater.
This Mummy
smiles less and less.

I've been going

to school for three weeks now.
Mummy keeps saying,

Give it time. You'll get used to it.
Look at Anna. She's doing okay.

She's wrong.
I hate everything about it.
And I think Anna
hates school
as much as I do.
She just doesn't say anything.

Mummy's making

potato chops
for supper tonight.
I love the meat
and potato patties,
but they're even more
delicious with HP Brown sauce.

I need eggs,
Mummy says.

   And more HP sauce,
I add.

She gives
Anna and me
three pounds,
and we head off,
coins jingling
in our pockets.

The Grocer's

Three boys
stand outside
the door,
shooting us
nasty looks.

Go back home,
one of the boys says.
I stop and glare at him.

    Ignore them.
    Anna grabs my arm and pushes me inside.

You get the sauce and I'll get the eggs,
Anna tells me.

I meet Anna
at the register.
Behind us,
two women
wrinkle their noses
and step back.
I pretend
not to notice
and slowly shuffle
closer to them.
Haa!
Anna shoots
me her best
mummy-warning look.

More and more of **them** *moving in every day.*
The whole street smells like curry . . . disgusting.
My Alfred said they are taking all the jobs away
    from us.
The National Front wants to send them back.
I'm with them!

How rude!
I want to dump this bottle
of HP sauce right
on their heads.
I turn.
Anna grabs my arm,
holding it tightly.
We hand the checkout clerk our items.

    That will be two pounds, fifty.

Anna shakes the coins onto the counter to count.
Behind me I hear sighs and groans.

    Stupid Indians don't know how to count.

This time Anna isn't fast enough.
I spin around.

Shut up! You ugly old crows.

The women
stare at me shocked,
their eyes wide
and mouths hanging open.
The girl at the register
giggles.

156

Anna snatches our bag
and rushes out.
I hurry
to catch up.
Behind us,
I hear the three boys . . .

Run Paki! Run!

Run Paki! Run!

When Mummy hears

what happened,
she asks me . . .

When will you learn to control your temper?

She's not interested
in hearing what the
old ladies said
or the ugly words
the boys shouted.

You are too quick with your words.
It's going to get you into trouble.

I'm already in trouble,
I think to myself.

My Days at School

I arrive.
Nobody talks to me.
I have no friends.
Sanjeev and his buddies
push and bump me.
They dump their stuff
on my desk,
put snails and slugs
in my locker,
kick the back of my chair,
and break my pencils.
Kids give me nasty looks.
Mrs. Wright never calls on me.
I've stopped raising my hand.
I say nothing.
Kids whisper about me.
She's dumb.
She can't speak English.
She doesn't understand us.
But they're wrong—I do.
I hear everything they're saying.
And understand them, too.
I stand alone at recess.
I sit alone at lunch.
I walk through the halls
as if I'm invisible.
The best part
of school
is when
    it's
        over.

My Letter to Maggie

Dear Maggie,

I hope you haven't forgotten me.
You better not have!
I <u>desperately</u> need your help. NOW!
You have to get me out of here.

I thought the Guptas' house was
torture, but where we are now is so much worse.
It's like
living in
one of the bunkers on the RAF base.
My school is awful.
The kids are mean.
I miss you and Mark and want to come back.

PLEASE ask your mum if we can stay with you
until Daddy
gets here (because I still believe he's coming,
even if Mummy and
Anna don't).

    Please. Please. Pretty-please.

We don't have a phone, so you can't ring me.
Write as soon as you get this. I don't know if I
can survive much longer. This life
is sucking out
all of my Supremeness.

Your fun, fabulous friend,
VIVA

p.s. I promise to make you an honorary member
of my Supremes club
and teach you all their songs.
You just can't be Diana.

Trip to Grunwick

Mummy is
taking Anna and me
to Grunwick Laboratories.
We are two
excited sisters.
My entire body
bubbles
with eagerness.
We're going
to ride
on the tube.
The giant
underground python
that slithers
through dark tunnels.
It's what Daddy
calls the trains
travelling
deep beneath
the streets of London

Vibrations tickle
my feet.

    Clickety, clackety, clickety, clack.

Anna hugs me
from behind.
Crowds
huddle near
the edge
of the platform.

And then,
out of the darkness,
a light shines
and a train
flies into the station
with a tumbling,
twisting gust of wind
and screeches to a stop.
The door slides open and we get on!

Mum's job

is not
what I expected.
I had no idea
it took her
over an hour
to get to work.
I had no idea
she's squashed
in a large,
hot room
with lots
of other
women,
all shades of brown.
Indians,
Pakistanis,
Hindus,
squashed
for hours.

I want to
shout at her.
                    Quit!
Kampala Mummy
was Deputy Headmistress
of a school.
That Mummy
was feisty,
a go-getter.
A never-give-upper.
I need that Mummy.

            Where is she?

On the way home

we bump
into Mr. Singh.
His turban is
blue like the sky
in Kampala
and he always
has a smile
for Anna and me.
But today
there's no smile.
Only worried eyes.

You shouldn't be out with the girls,

he tells Mummy
and shoves a flyer
in her hands.

They're expecting trouble.
NF.
It's not safe.

What kind of trouble?
I want to know,
but Mummy's
taken off
like her feet
are being bitten
by red ants.

Three Boys

The same boys
that called
Anna and me names
are outside
the grocer's shop.
    Run Pakis. Run back home.
There's no way
Mummy's going
to let them
get off
without a good
scolding.
Her fingers tighten
around my hand.
    Ignore them,
she warns.
I don't understand.
Kampala Mummy never
let kids be disrespectful
when she was Deputy Headmistress.
So, why is it okay now?

    Run Paki Mummy.
    Run with your stupid kids.

Anger boils inside me.
Then explodes.
I wrench free
from Mummy
and whip around.
We're Indian.
Not Pakistani.
Now who's STUPID?

Go to your room!

Mummy says.

    But . . . it's not fair.
I sputter.
    You did nothing.
    I had to say something.

Mummy falls silent
and stares at me.
I've stopped time.
Her hand freezes.
I see the milk jug
trembling slightly
over her teacup
and I wish
I could
take back
my words.

Alone

in my room,
the boys' words
choke Diana's voice
and fill my head
with their ugliness.
I see the newspaper.

NO MORE ASIANS.

SEND THE REFUGEES HOME.

It's no use.
I can't pretend.
I am the refugee
that nobody wants.
I take a breath
and think
of all the words
that rhyme with

REFUGEE

Deputy

Beauty

Ghee

See

Me

SEE ME!

The Colored Girl

They don't see me.
All they see is a girl
with skin the color
of dark tea,
with eyes
brown as roasted chestnuts,
with hair as dark as coal.

They don't see me.

They see another refugee
    from Uganda.

        A colored girl.

It's been two weeks

and there's still
no letter from Maggie.
She made me promise
to not forget her
and she's
forgotten
me.

The Brick

It arrives
with an

        explosion,

shattering the
        still
        of night.

Mummy screams.

Anna and I
scramble
out of bed
and charge
into the sitting room.

Shards
of glass
lay everywhere
and there's a hole
in the front window.

The culprit
is a brick
wrapped in paper.

A cold wind
blows
into the room
like an unwanted
guest you
can't get rid of.

The NF

While I sweep
up the broken glass,
Mummy and Anna
help Mr. Singh
cover the hole
with cardboard
and newspaper.

His sitting room
was also attacked.
Guess the bricks
in London
only like
windows
that Indians
look out.

I lift the lid
off the bin
and there,
among banana peels
and eggshells,
is the—

       THE BRICK

The letters
NF
are on the paper
wrapped around it.

   National Front

I sneak the paper

into the bathroom to read.

Make Britain Great Again
Stop Immigration
British People Before Immigrants
British Jobs For British Workers
Send Them Back

I don't know
who the National Front is,
but I do know
they don't
want me here.

I do know
that I don't like this feeling
of not being wanted.

Let me in.
It's Anna.
I open the door
And pull her inside.
Look!
I show the NF paper.
Mr. Singh warned Mummy about them.
We have to do something.

Anna snatches
the papers out
of my hands and
throws them to the floor.

Haven't you done enough?
When you talk back and yell at them, it makes
things worse.
Why can't you ignore them? Walk away.

I want to walk away from Anna and this stupid
conversation.

Hateful People

When I tell Mummy

    I hate hateful people

she tells me that the Bible says . . .
    to turn the other cheek,
    to be kind to your neighbors,
    to love your enemies.

I think about the
person that
threw the brick
at our window.
The brick
that could have
hit Mummy.

I hate that person
and I don't care
what God
thinks.

The next morning

I find Anna
in bed,
reading.

 I'm not going to school,

she says
when I ask
why she's not ready.

 It's my breathing.

My lie detector is blaring.
But what can I do?
I wish I could stay home too.

I walk to school

alone,
scared of my
own shadow.
I think about
the flyer,
the NF,
and who
threw the brick.

What if
the person goes
to my school?

What if
they are
watching me,
right now?
Waiting.

I clutch
my school satchel
to my chest
and run
not feeling
very courageous
or Diana Supremeness.

School

Suddenly, I'm
not invisible.
Heads turn.
Eyes follow me.
Whispers chase after me.

> NF
> *Too many of them.*
> *Keep Britain for the British.*

Sanjeev leans
over and I
ready myself
for his usual attack,
but he surprises me.

> *Daddy told me what happened. It's wrong,*
> *what they did. Jerks!*

I'm shocked.
Sanjeev being nice?
It's the most
he's said to me
since I started
at his school.

I'm seriously gobsmacked.

GOBSMACKED: gob·smacked/'gäb,smakt/
to be utterly astonished; astounded
*British slang . . . had to make up my own definition,
but I think Daddy will like it.

North Star

My hope,
that used
to shine
as bright as
the North Star,
is starting
to fade.
There's no news about Daddy.
Maggie never wrote back.
I hate my school.
I hate my life.
I say my night prayers
but my heart
isn't in it.

God has forgotten me.

I Love Saturday

No school.
No work for Mummy.
Fresh hot chapatis.

Chapatis and jam
are Daddy's favorite.
Mine too.

Today's are
going to be
extra yummy.
Mrs. Singh brought
over some guava jam.

Saturday morning chapatis
are going to be
super-duper delicious.
YUM!!!

Knocking
interrupts our
scrummy breakfast.
It's the neighbor
from upstairs.
She hands Mummy
an envelope.

Sorry. This was delivered to me by mistake.

It's a telegram.
My tummy clenches.

The Telegram

Detained in Entebbe by police. Missed my flight. Couldn't get word to you. Leaving tomorrow. Arriving Heathrow on January 23. Can't wait to see you.
With Love.

Diana

croons in my ear.
I sing along
to her song . . .

"Someday, We'll Be Together"

Anna joins me.
We sing
waving our arms,
shaking our hips,
our happiness
filling every space
of the tiny flat.

Something Is Wrong

Mummy hasn't moved.
She's sitting
on the wobbly
kitchen chair staring
at the telegram.

    Mummy, what's wrong?

Anna asks.
She doesn't seem to hear,
So I try.

    Mummy, why aren't you happy?

Her mind is someplace else.
Her eyes are sad.
I don't understand.
This is good news.
Fantastic news.
So why
is Mummy's face
a map of worry lines?
Anna drops my hand.
I look at her.

    What's wrong?

The date,
Anna says.
January 23rd.
That was
two days ago.
And just like that
my happy moment
    is annihilated.

The Same Old Routine

Mummy goes to work.
Anna and I go to school.
It's like the telegram never arrived.

Something has to change.
I have to make it happen.
If I don't, I'll go absolutely

C
R
A
Z
Y.

I need a plan.

What Would Diana Do?

HOPE.

Diana's mama
told her
never give up.
Hold on to hope.

Daddy is a big
hope holder.
He always
tells the story of how he
never gave up when
Mummy turned him
down for a date.

He held on to hope
that one day
he'd change her mind.
And he did.

I look at my wings.
I'm not going to just
HOPE
to find Daddy.
I am going to
make it happen.

Daddy is probably
somewhere
in London
looking
for me.
I am going to soar
on my wings
and find him.

February 1973

I've got
my wings.
Courage.
Strength.

Today's the Day

I hate lying
to Mummy
and Anna.
But I'm doing this.
Hope is alive.
Sparkly.
Beating in my heart.
I've got my wings.
Courage.
Strength.
I'm going to London
to find Daddy.

The Plan

I walk with Anna
to school,
trying not to look
super-duper rushed.
She takes forever
to walk inside the building
but the second she does,
I spin around
and head straight
to the High Street.
My heart thuds
madly-crazily
beneath my ribs.

While waiting for the bus,
I think through my plan.

1) Bus to Victoria Station.
2) Get directions to Heathrow.
3) Find BOAC terminal.
4) Ask if Daddy arrived on any of their flights in the
   last few days.
5) Make it back before Mummy gets home from work.

What if something goes wrong?

The thought settles
on my shoulders
with the weight
of a thousand
bricks.
Maybe I should have
told Anna, I mutter out loud.

> *Told me what?*
> It's Anna!

Sister Trouble

What are you doing
here? I ask.

> What are **you** doing here?
> I knew you were up to something
> so I waited and followed.

You need to go.   *Why?*

I'm going to the airport
to find out about Daddy.

> *Does Mummy know*
> *what you're doing?*

(This is why I don't tell Anna
stuff. She's a tattletale.)

> *I knew it! She has no idea.*

I'll be back before she gets home.

> *Good! I'll come too.*

What? No! You can't.   *Why not?*

B-b-because . . .
(Darn. I can't think of
a good reason.)

> *Perfect.*
> Anna hooks her arm
> in mine and smiles.
> *What's the plan?*

I sigh.

> *Don't look so grumpy. It will be just like*
> *the adventures in my Enid Blyton books.*

190

Bus No. 5

Red double-decker buses
trundle
up and down
the street.

> We need the No. 5.
> > *It's turning right now, Anna says.*

> You sure you want to come? I try one last time.
> > *Yup! You're not getting rid of me that easily.*

The bus pulls to the curb.
I grip the metal pole
and take a breath
to steady my quivering knees.
One small step at a time.
I climb up,
and find two seats
in the back.

> We need to be able to hop off quickly, I tell Anna.

The conductor checks our travel passes.

> Can you tell us when we get to Victoria Station? I ask.
> > *Sure think, luv, he says.*

Curious eyes
settle upon
Anna and me.
My stomach twists.
I look away.

London Sites

Look it's . . .
Big Ben
Parliament
River Thames
Anna announces
as the sites slide
past the window.

Instead of excitement,
a terrible ache gnaws
at me.

I squeeze my wings for courage.

It's so easy to get lost in this city.
London is
　　　HUGE.

Victoria Station

The map has
so many
colored lines,
weaving in and out,
with squares
and circles,
strange sounding
stations.

> Anna narrows her eyes. *You do know where we're
> going, right?*

I nod and
bite my lip,
eyeing the
escalators,
long winding corridors,
ticket booths, and
people everywhere.

What was I thinking?

We need help!

People hurry

in every direction,
their eyes fixed ahead.
I gather courage
to stop someone
and spot
a lady with a smile
like Miss Robinson
from RAF.
Anna is too nervous
to speak, so
I talk for both of us.
I swallow hard,
preparing my words.
                    Excuse me—
                        No. Get away.
The lady rushes off.
I keep trying
and get
headshakes,
scowls,
no,
sorry can't help,
don't know.

How are we going to get to Heathrow if nobody will
help us?

I can't give up,

not when
I've come this far.
Not when I
told Anna that
I had this all planned out.

I think of the song
Daddy and I sing
whenever we start
hunting for a
word in Big Blue.

Undeterred, we'll find the word,
A-hunting we will go.

I change it
Undeterred, ~~we'll find the word,~~
   I'll find the way—

Anna's hand
suddenly
pulls me back.

Oh, no!
Trouble ahead.
The Miss Robinson lookalike
is standing with a
police officer
and pointing
   at us.

    There they are. The two troublemakers. Do something.

THIS IS NOT GOOD!

What are we going to do?

Anna asks, in a panicky voice.

        Shhhh! I'm thinking.
I look around,
blinking rapidly.
We're surrounded by
multiple lanes,
multiple trains,
multiple exits.
We don't have much time.
The officer and horrible lady
are getting closer.
WWDD
What Would Diana Do?

      I've got it.

Follow me, I tell Anna.
I glance up at the train schedule,
pretending to understand
the flipping and turning
numbers and letters.
Mustering all my confidence,
which is about the size of a pea,
I walk straight toward them,

      SMILING

On the count of three, run,
I whisper.
I wait until they're about five feet away
and reach for Anna's hand.
One. Two. Three. RUN!

We dash down the lane.
Hop onto the closest train
and collapse into the first seat.

SAFE!

I did it!

I take a deep breath
to calm my racing heart.
Outside the window,
the officer is shaking his head.
The horrible lady is waving her arms.
Ha!

Anna looks at me.
We burst into fits
of sister giggles.
The sound fills the air
like the fireworks
on Guy Fawkes night.

As soon as they leave we'll get off,
I tell Anna.

We watch.
We wait.
The train jerks.
Anna's eyes widen.

Wait, what's happening?

Noooo!
We're moving.

197

Sister Storm

The train gathers speed,
moving faster and faster.
Anna whirls around
in a storm of anger.

What was I thinking coming with you?
I should have known we'd end up in a mess.
You can't do anything right!

> I can't believe Anna is getting
> all high and mighty with me.
> Th-th-that's not fair! I sputter.

I should have gone home and phoned Mummy.

> That's right. Tattle to Mummy.
> Then both of you can go back to your
> fake life and forget all about Daddy.

What are you talking about?
We haven't forgotten about Daddy!

> I don't see you and Mummy trying to
> find out what happened to him?

Well I'm here now, aren't I?

> I wish you weren't.

Me too!

The train stops.
Anna and I freeze.
We look at one another
and make a dash
for the door.

Lost

We are surrounded by
a dense cluster
of dull brick
and concrete buildings
under a quickly darkening sky.
I shiver as the crisp air
wraps its chilly fingers
around me.
I glance at Anna,
worried about her lungs
and breathing.

> *I'm freezing, Anna grumbles.*
> *This was a stupid idea.*

I'm starting to agree.
Getting on and off
the train
going in different directions
has me completely
turned around.
I have no idea where we are.
I want to
fly home,
fold up my wings,
and hide.

Strangers

Are you lost?

The voice is as deep as a bass drum.
Anna clutches my arm.
We spin around and come
face-to-face with two police.
The man wears a black helmet hat
like Officer Graham.
The woman has on a pot-shaped hat.
Panicky flutters grip me tightly.
Will they arrest us?
Take us to jail?
My heart pounds.
What if we never see Mummy again?
Or Daddy?
My voice is lost.
Anna's too.
They look at us curiously.

   Where are your parents?
The woman speaks softly.
   Why don't you come along with us?
Kindness shines from her eyes.
   *We'll get you a nice cup of tea and sandwich
   and see if we can find out where you belong.*

Food and warmth.
I speak to Anna with my eyes.
She blinks and nods.
We follow the officers
silently.

Questions

What's your name?   Viva. This is my sister, Anna.

Did you run away?   We shake our heads.

How did you get here?

Where are your mum and dad?

What's your address?   I shrug.
(My address in Kampala
pops in my head.)

Do you know where you live?   Southall, Anna says.

Where in Southall?   We both shrug.

What's your telephone number?
(We share a phone in the building.
Neither of us knows the number.)

The officers glance nervously at each other when
we don't respond.

Tea and Sandwiches

Are you going to eat that other sandwich?

> Anna gives me one of her exasperated sister
> sighs. *I can't believe you.*

What? I'm hungry.

> She hands me the other half of her cheese sandwich.
> *Mummy is probably home, wondering where we are.*
> *Panicked.*

Guilt pokes at me.
They'll figure out something.
I glance at the officers.

> Anna shakes her head.
> *I should have dragged you back to school.*
> *Not agreed to your crazy plan.*

I bite and chew.
Sip my tea.
Chew some more.
We are surrounded
by officers and it
makes me think
of Officer Graham.
That's it!
Why didn't I think of this before?

I tell the kind lady officer
about RAF Greenham and
Officer Graham.
She scribbles down his name.

I can do things right!
I tell Anna.
Officer Graham will help us.

Oh, no! Officer Graham is mad.

Marching
Angry
Displeased

MAD.
He fires questions
one after the other
even after I tell him about Daddy and the
telegram.

What were you thinking leaving the school?

Why would you do such a thing?

Do you know how worried everyone is?

Why didn't you tell your Mum?

*What if something happened to
the two of you?*

As his voice
gets louder
I shrink
in
my
chair.

Long Drive

A sharp gust
of cold air
strikes as
we step
out of the
station.
It creeps
under my coat
and I shiver.

A very cross Officer Graham
stomps to his car
and Anna and I trudge behind him.
It feels like my world
        is crashing
                around me.

The Drive Home

I talked to your mum.

Is she okay? Anna asks.

She was really worried.

We didn't mean to worry her,
I say, wishing
this car ride
was over.

*Your mum's doing her best. It can't be easy
without your dad.*

That's why we were trying to find him.

*Let the grownups worry about the big stuff. Like
finding your dad. It's tough on your mum right now.
She can't be worried about the two of you.
You have to help her. I think that's what your dad
would want, don't you?*

I feel Anna's hand wrap around mine.
She squeezes my fingers.
I can't talk because suddenly I'm closer than ever
to crying.

Mummy is waiting outside

when we pull up.
I am going
to be grounded
for life.
I get ready
for the longest
lecture ever.
Instead,
Mummy pulls
Anna and me
into a rib-crushing
hug,
and holds on
like she'll
never
let
go.

Three days later,

Anna wakes up with watery eyes and a fever.
My head feels like it's about to explode.
She moans.
> *You have a fever,*
> Mummy says.
> *I don't know what you were thinking,*
> *gallivanting at night.*
> *Where is your common sense?*

It was my idea, I tell Mummy.

> Disappointment grows on her face.
> *Your sister has to be careful. You know that.*

> *It's not Viva's fault, Anna jumps in.*
> *She didn't want me to go. I made her.*

I can't believe Anna is standing up for me.

> *I'm really disappointed with both of you.*
> Mummy's words hurt worse than any
> punishment or scolding.

I sit with Anna
while Mummy goes
to check if Mrs. Singh
can watch Anna.
My sister tucks her head
into my shoulder.

> *This isn't your fault. I really wanted to go with you.*
> *I always miss out because I have to be careful.*

Later that day,

when Mummy comes back
from the hospital
without Anna,
panic clutches my heart
and squeezes so tightly,
I can hardly breathe.
Anna kept getting worse
so Mummy took her to emergency.

> They are keeping her a few days to be safe.
> She has a viral infection—meningitis.

Mummy's words
crash down
upon me.

This is my fault.

I never meant

for this to happen.
I'm so sorry.
I just want Anna
to get better
and come home.
Wrapped tightly
in Mummy's arms
the weight
of my sadness,
disappointment,
guilt, and missing Daddy
bursts and all the tears
I've been holding in
gush like Victoria Falls.

   I just wanted to find Daddy.

I say between sobs.

   I can't live without him.
   I want Anna to come home.
   I want my family.
   I want Daddy back.

Anna is home

and bossier than ever.
Mummy said she can
stay home until term break.
LUCKY HER!
Mrs. Singh pops in
and watches Anna
during the day.

After school, it's my turn.
That's when I turn into
Cinderella and
Anna is one of the stepsisters . . .

Where's my hot water bottle?
I need a cup of tea.
Make me a sandwich.
Get me my book.

Aghhhhhh!

Two weeks later

a clicking noise wakes me.
I lie really still,
eyes wide open,
and listen for it again.

Nothing.

Next to me,
Anna is a curled lump,
hogging the covers
like she does every night.
I don't care.
It's good to have her home.
Mummy softly snores
on the narrow cot opposite.

My tummy growls,
demanding food.
I creep out of bed
careful not
to wake them.

BRRR!

I spot the culprit
on the floor
and do my best
to stick the cardboard
back over the
gaping hole
in the front window.

On my way
to the kitchen,
a paper
catches my eye.
That's the noise I heard.
Someone pushing papers
through the letterbox.
In the dim light,
I recognize
the red, white, and blue
NF logo.

The National Front
is about hate
and I hate them.

There's also a magazine—*Spearhead*.
The front page reads:
Make Britain Great Again.
I crumple
the papers and shove
them back through
the letterbox.

    UNWANTED

        UNPLEASANT

            UNREAD

I Hate Hateful Words

While Mummy and Anna
are at her doctor check-up,
I finish vacuuming.
It doesn't make a difference.
The flat still looks dingy and used,
even after we tidy.

The vacuum whirls, caught
on something.
I peek under Mum's cot.
It's a stack of papers.
I scoot further
under the cot and
drag them out.

No way!
It's a bunch of flyers.
A whole bunch,
not just four or five.
Some handwritten.
Some printed.
All with the same message.

WE DON'T WANT YOU!

I don't understand.
If Mummy knew,
WHY didn't she
get us out of Southall?

WHY didn't she protect us?

I confront Mummy as soon as she steps through the door.

Did you know about these flyers?
                          Where did you find them?

Under your bed.
                  I was protecting you and Anna.

How?
You let them call us names
and did nothing.
                      Sometimes you need to know
                          when to be quiet.

You were quiet and they threw a brick at us.
                              That's not fair.

You said we'd be okay.
If Daddy was here, he'd say something.
He'd make them STOP calling us names.
He'd have kept us safe.
I wish he were here instead of you.

I know I've gone

too far.
I want to undo
that last second and
take back my words.
But that's impossible.
It's like a volcano.
Once it explodes,
you can't put the lava back inside.
I think there's something
wrong with me.
Anna never has this problem.
Neither does Ella.
Good, polite, well-behaved Indian daughters.
Why do I always say the wrong thing?
Why do I always do the wrong thing?

        What.

        Is.

        Wrong.

        With.

        Me?

Guilt

I wake to soft crying.
Anna is sleeping.
Mummy's cot is empty.
Quietly I crawl out of bed
and creep to the sitting room.
Mummy sits on the sofa,
her hands pressed to her eyes
and her shoulders quivering.

    Mummy, I'm really sorry for yelling at you.

Her eyes immediately widen
on seeing me.
She reaches for my hand.
I sit beside her.

    Viva, I know it hasn't been easy since we moved
    to Southall.
        I hate feeling like I'm not wanted.

    That's why I hid those flyers from you and Anna.
    You shouldn't have to feel bad for who you are.
        I didn't feel like that at RAF Greenham.
        They were nice there.

    I know and I can't promise anything, but I am
    trying to figure out something.
        I wrote a letter to Maggie and asked if we could
        stay with her in Newbury, but I never heard back.

    It's been hard without your father, for all of us.
    I never thought we'd be separated.

I hug Mummy tightly,
because whenever I'm upset,
Mummy and Daddy hug me.
So that's what I do.

We sit together on the sofa,
hand-in-hand,
my head on her shoulder.

Cardboard covers the hole
the brick left in our window,
but the wind whistles
a reminder of the
        ugliness,
        viciousness,
        and hate.
I do not want
to be a part of it
and will try harder
to lessen my volcanic
eruptions.

217

Three weeks later

everything changes.
When Anna and I
get home from school
Mummy is waiting.
Which is weird
because she never gets
home from work
before us.
A wave of
fear grips me
in its icy clutches.
Anna grabs my hand.
I can't breathe.

We're moving,
Mummy tells us.
>   WHAT?
>   Anna and I say at the same time.

We're moving to Newbury.

This time,
I'm the one
giving the
rib-crushing
hug, never
wanting to
let go.

Here's What Happened

Maggie stapled my letter
to her math homework
and turned it in to her teacher.

I should have written to Mark!

Anyway, when she got it back,
she showed it to her mum.
Mrs. Mackay showed it to Mrs. Robinson.
Mrs. Robinson showed it to Officer Graham.
He told them about my trip to London to look for
Daddy.
And the hateful BRICK.

So . . .
When Mummy telephoned Officer Graham,
they already had a PLAN
to help us.
All because of MY letter.

Now we are moving back!

I am NOT going to miss . . .

the cold, ugly flat
the three mean boys on the High Street.
the lonely school
the angry bricks
the hate flyers
the go-away stares from strangers.

March 1973

Good
to
Be
Back

Maggie

I'm barely out of the car
when Maggie barrels out
of her house,
screaming
so loudly
so long
so shrill
that I'm afraid every dog
in the neighborhood
is going to start howling.

Mark

You've been gone for eight weeks.
That's forty days.
Nine-hundred sixty hours.
You're finally back.
What took you so long?

Good to Be Back

Words fly
out of Maggie's mouth so fast
that I worry she's going
to run out of air
and pass out.

> I'm so glad you wrote, 'cause I missed your
> call and then Mummy forgot to get your
> number and I couldn't ring you back. I can't
> believe I stapled your letter to my math
> homework. I'm so sorry. Doesn't matter you
> are here now and I have so much to tell you.
> School is okay. Nothing new, well except Mrs.
> Bing is having a baby and I kind of failed my
> last math test.

Not kind of. You did fail,
Mark jumps in.
Maggie shoots him a dirty look
and continues . . .

> Mum has me taking piano lessons and my
> teacher is horrible. She stands behind me
> poking me in the back to sit straight and
> hits my wrist with a ruler when I don't keep
> them straight, which only makes me hit
> more wrong notes, but I can play "Baa Baa
> Black Sheep" with no mistakes. The base is
> crazy full. Buses keep coming with more and
> more people from Uganda. I've met a couple
> of new kids too. Oh, but don't worry none of
> them are as great as you.

Maggie jumps over
and throws her arms
around me.

Anna rolls her eyes,
but I can tell
my sister is happy
to be back,
especially when Maggie
grabs her to join
in the hug.

Serendipity

It was *serendipity* that Maggie's teacher found
your letter,
Mark says.
He hands me a paper.
For your wordbook.

> **SERENDIPITY: ser·en·dip·i·te /ˌserən'dipəti/**
> occurring or discovering by chance in a happy or
> beneficial way

Ser-en-dip-i-ty
I can't wait
to add this
to my wordbook.
It was serendipity
that I found
Maggie and Mark.

Supper is . . .

crispy fish
potatoey chips
tangy malt vinegar
fizzy pop
greasy fingers
salty lips
stuffed tummies
non-stop talking
laughter
giggles
smiles
HAPPINESS
Until.
It.
Isn't.

Perfect Day Ruined

What?
I don't believe it.
It can't be true.
We are staying with Mrs. Robinson.
Not Miss Robinson.
Not Mrs. McGee.
Not Maggie and Mark.
MRS. ROBINSON!
Gloomy
Growly
Frosty
Cranky
       Mrs. Robinson.

     WHY ME?

Welcome

Mrs. Robinson opens the door,
peers down at me,
her pale blue eyes set deep
in her lined face.
Her brown hair sits
in curled lumps
reminding me
of short pork sausages.

Welcome. Please come in.

I follow her
to the sitting room.
Stop.
Stare.
The walls
are bright orange.
It's like we've been
swallowed
by a giant mango.
There's no sign of
a Mr. Robinson
and I don't ask.

Settling In

I share a room with Anna
and it is awesome.
It makes me
feel cozy,
sparkly,
and safe.

Bedtime

I'm talking to God again.
I join Anna
in our nighttime
prayers
and thank God
that I am no longer
in Southall.

Anna screams.
I spin around ready
to do battle with
the alien creature
standing in the doorway.
It's Mrs. Robinson.
Head in curlers.
Face covered in cold cream.
Wrapped in a fluffy dressing gown.
Alien creature.

I have a small gift for you.

What?
Mrs. Robinson with gifts?

*Your mum told me about Christmas and I wanted
to get you something.
It's small.*

She hands Anna a bag.
Inside is a new book by Enid Blyton.
The Famous Five Go Adventuring Again
Oh great.

Just when I was finally getting my sister back,
she's going to spend all of her time
with Julian, Dick, Anne, George,
and the dog, Timothy,
on one of their adventures.
And there she goes . . .
Nose buried on page one.

Open yours.

Mrs. Robinson holds out my bag.
Oh no!
Not a book, too.
I smile widely
hoping it doesn't look fake.
I look inside the bag.
Seriously?
Oh My God!
*(Sorry God. I know I'm not supposed to say your
name in vain.)*

But this is . . .
Amazing
Astonishing
Stupefying.
It's a Mini Blue.

Mrs. Robinson got me
the mini *Oxford Dictionary*.
Inside it says . . .

To Viva,

Every logophile deserves their
own dictionary.
   Happy hunting.
   Mrs. Robinson

What's a logophile?

   It's a person who loves words.

Thank you.
It's the best gift ever.
I mean it, too.
She looks at me
with watery blue eyes.

   I thought you and Anna deserved something special.

232

Question

Who
is
THIS
Mrs. Robinson?

What has she done with the old one?

The next morning

Mrs. Robinson calls me downstairs.

There's someone to see you.

I just know it's Leroy.
He heard I'm back.
As I climb downstairs
I see scruffy tennis shoes,
     brown corduroys,
     a striped shirt.
The stairs creak.
I stop.
He's singing my song:
"Ain't No Mountain High Enough"
My Supremes!

That isn't Leroy.
I bend down and peek.

It's Officer Graham.

My heart soars
like a kite
and so do my legs,
leaping off the steps
and right into
his arms.
I put all my
thank yous
into one
humongous
    HUG.

Conversation with Officer Graham

That day I picked you up, your mum told me about
the telegram from your father.
    Did you find out anything?

I spoke to someone at the airport from the
British Overseas Airways Corporation.
    And?
    Was he on the flight?
    Is he here?

Yes! Your father was on the flight and he arrived
in London.
But that's all I know.

I'm on my feet.
I grab Anna,
swing and sing
"Someday We'll Be Together."
in full Diana fabulousness.

Pan in hand.
Scowling.
Glowering.
Mrs. Robinson appears from the kitchen.
My fabulousness is chapati flat.
This is the Mrs. Robinson
I remember.
She's back!

A Couple of Weeks Later

We are living in Newbury,
with Mrs. Robinson
who isn't so bad, after all.
And Newbury is a hundred,
million, quadrillion times
better than Southall.

Maggie and Mark live five minutes away.
Four minutes if I run.
Three minutes, if I run super-duper fast.

Mummy's teaching Form 7 on RAF base.
Anna is in her class.
I'm not. Thank you, God.
I don't think I'm the kind of student
Mummy wants in her class.

Leroy is nowhere to be seen.
I'm think he's forgotten about me.

On weekends, Anna and I help Miss Robinson
in the common room.
I hide the ugly newspapers from the Indians.
The ones that say . . .

> *No More Asians*
> *Keep Britain for the British*
> *Send Them Back!*

And the best happening is . . .

Daddy is somewhere in London!

I'm not afraid

walking alone
from the bus stop
to Mrs. Robinson's house.
I don't look over my shoulder
for flying bricks
or worry
about ugly words
chasing after me.

People smile
when I pass,
say hello,
nod.
I like it here.
I will miss this London
when Daddy finally
finds us and
we fly off
to Canada
to start our new life.

Unsettled

I slide the key in the lock
open the door and stop.
What's that noise?
Crying.
Soft.
Quiet.
Sobs.

I tiptoe
into the kitchen.
Mrs. Robinson sits
with her face
in her hands.
Her shoulders
moving in waves
up and down.
Photos
lay scattered
on the table.

I slide into the chair
next to her.
Unnoticed.
There's a photo of a man
holding a baby.
Another of a lady
splashing in the sea.

Then I see the one
closest to Mrs. Robinson.
A wedding photo.
    Is that you?

Mrs. Robinson gasps.

She rubs her eyes and face.
Stares at me.
Silent.
> That's Ronnie. It was our wedding day.

She picks
up the photo.
Tears roll
down her cheeks.
> He died in World War II.
> His birthday's next week.

I hold
Mrs. Robinson's hand
and sit quietly
in her bold,
mango orange kitchen.
> He sang wherever he went.
> Bit like you.

I think I would have liked him.
> I think he would have liked you, too.

I stare at the photo
of the young Mrs. Robinson,
laughing,
eyes shining.
Maybe her too-sad heart
simply forgot how to smile.
Missing someone you love can do that.
I know.
And I've only been missing Daddy
for a couple of months.
Not a lifetime.

Mrs. Robinson's Happiness Project

Maggie, Mark, and Anna agree.
Great idea!
Ideas spark like fireworks.

> *We'll do it at our house.* (Maggie)

> *Chocolate is the best.* (Mark)

> *Strawberry and vanilla is better.* (Anna)

We compromise.
Vanilla cake with
Chocolate frosting.
Strawberries on top.
We'll meet at 3:00 PM. (me)

> *Will we have enough time?* (Maggie)

> Plenty. Mrs. Robinson and Mum get home
> around 5:00 PM. (me)

> *3:00 PM. Hmmmm. That's cutting it close.* (Mark)

The average cake takes 2.5 hours to bake and cool.
Baking and cooling times will vary depending on the
size of your cake.
Do we cool it at room temperature (60–90 minutes)
or in the fridge (30 minutes)?
Then, we need time after it cools to spread the
frosting and place the strawberries.

STOP! (Anna, Maggie, and me)

How do you know this stuff? (Anna)

Because he is Mark. (Maggie and me)

Laughing (Mark, Anna, Maggie, and me)
We agree to meet at 2:00 PM.

Cooking Catastrophe

Measured wrong.
Forgot to add eggs.
Added eggs at the end.
Lumpy batter.
Running out of time.
Didn't butter and flour pan before baking.

Agghhhhh!

Waiting for the Cake to Bake

What was it like in Southall?
Maggie asks.

Awful! Anna says.

I hated Southall, I tell Maggie.
There were signs on the shop windows:
NO MORE ASIANS.
Angry, mean glares.

It's the National Front,
Mark joins in.
They want Britain for the British.
They want to keep Britain white.

I don't get it, Maggie says.
Viva's brown. I'm white.
We're different, but we're still people.
People are the same.

Not to them, Mark adds.
Color matters.

That's dumb!
Grownups can be so stupid.

It wasn't just the NF, Anna says. It was
kids too.
These three boys yelled rude things to us
all the time.
But Viva showed them!

I yelled and shouted back using my Diana
Ross lungs.

Good for you! Maggie says.
I'd have done the same.

I knew Maggie would understand.
She's that kind of friend.
She gets me.

Burnt Cake

We glance at the clock.

Oh, no! The cake!

We run to the kitchen.
Mark grabs oven mitts.
I yank open the oven.
A heavy burnt smell
prickles my nose.
We've burnt the cake.
No problem!
Anna says.

Instead of a cake,
we've scooped
the non-burnt bits
into paper muffin molds,
mixed in sliced strawberries,
and topped it with
frosting.

SPECTACULAR.

Little cups of happiness.

SURPRISE!

Mrs. Robinson's scowly face
takes in everything.
Balloons.
Streamers.
Muffin cakes.
Nibbles.
Me.

It's a birthday party for Mr. Robinson,

I tell her and wait.
Mrs. Robinson's face
softens and then
crumples into sobs.

This is the nicest thing anyone has done for me.

She pulls me
into a squeeeezy hug
and places a little kiss
on the top
of my head.

Mark puts a record
on the player
and Diana Ross bursts
into the sitting room.

Mrs. Robinson sings
like she's one
of the Supremes
and she's wearing
the same smile
she had on in the
wedding photo with
Mr. Robinson.
    My idea worked!

Star Wishes

We sit side by side,
Mrs. Robinson and me,
in the cool night
staring up
at the smattering
of stars.

She leans over.
You see that star over there.
She points up.
*I think my Ronnie watches over me from behind that
star.*
I was lonely and he sent you.

I'm glad he did,
I tell her.

Me too, Viva.
She smiles at me through teary eyes.

Airstrip

I'm with Maggie
at the airstrip
watching the airmen
unload the post
from the plane
when a jeep pulls up
and stops.

> *Well, look who it is?*
> *Howdy, Lil' Diana. What are you doing here?*

Leroy smiles
his dimples winking
and eyes sparkling.
I jump up,
excited,
then remember
I'm mad at him.
I quickly scowl,
and put on my best frosty glare.

> *Whoa. What's that look for?*
> *he asks.*

I don't answer.

> *She's mad at you because you didn't come see her,*
> *Maggie says.*

> *Lil' Diana. That pains me because . . .*
> *Leroy stands up in the jeep*
> *And belts out . . .*

"My World Is Empty Without You."

No.
Not the Supremes.
It's taking every
single ounce of super
mega strength not to sing along.
Maggie is up
dancing,
swinging,
and singing
my favorite song.

Leroy jumps out
of the jeep
and goes down
on one knee.

> I can't sing alone,
> I can't carry on.

My frostiness
is melting
like the icing
on Mrs. Robinson's cupcakes.
It's hard work
staying mad at Leroy.
I'm getting weaker. Weaker.
Aggghh!
I can't do it any longer.
My inner Diana Ross
explodes.

We sing together.
The RAF Supremes.
Maggie,
Leroy,
and me.

Officer Graham Has News

Daddy was here.
Right here in London.
But
Now.
He.
Is.
Gone.

All because of this word . . .

EXPIRE

Who knew six letters
could yield such
power?

Mini-Blue knew.
p. 109

> **EXPIRE: ex·pire /ik'spī(ə)r/**
> cease to be valid, as a document, authorization,
> or agreement, typically after a fixed period of time

Expired Papers

It's why
Daddy
was taken
to a Detention Center
when he got
off the plane.

It's why
Daddy
couldn't stay
in London.

It's why
Daddy
got on a plane
to America and
not to Canada.

It's why we
can't fly
to meet him.
(Our travel vouchers expired)

It's why I
won't be living
in Canada with Ella.

EXPIRED PAPERS!

I feel like I'm going to expire
from a broken heart.

    EXPIRE: ex·pire /ik'spī(ə)r/
    to die, as a person

A Good Cry

My inside is
bursting.
Full with
too many feelings
pressing
into my heart.
Sadness.
Anger.
Fear.
I grab my wordbook
and start ripping,
page
after page.

HAPPINESS

ELATION   **JOY**

JUBILATION

Anna grabs the book
out of my hands.

STOP!

My body trembles.
Sobs come in waves.

Mummy rubs

soothing circles
on my back
and my sobs
quiet.
We sit
side by side,
the wetness
on her cheeks
blending
with my tears.
Her arms
around both
Anna and me.

School Project

I
have
to make a
chart for school
telling about my family.
A family tree.
Miss Robinson gives me red poster
paper and some markers and I start listing
all of my family—Granny and Grandpa, aunts,
uncles, cousins. We all used to be together and
now we're not. And I don't know if we ever will be
again. I look at the names of my family—Daddy,
Mummy, Anna, and me. We used to be a family of
four. Not three. I want things to go back to like
they were before, when I was a family of four with
Mummy
Daddy
Anna
Me.

A week later, Mummy has news.

Daddy is safe in New York,
she tells us.
A Jewish organization, HIAS, sponsored him
and that's how he ended up in New York.
Everything is okay.

Anger and fear
rush through me.
My inside volcano
bubbles again
and I can't hold it in.
It erupts.

OKAY?
Nothing is okay,
I shout.

Daddy's in New York.
We're in England.
Two different countries.
Two different continents.
An ocean between us.
NOT together.

How is THIS okay?

We're doing the best we can.
Mummy's voice sounds weary.
Not okay.

Anna glares.
I glare back,
but guilt pokes at me.

I don't know how

to keep
my mouth shut.

       Flying

                   Whizzing

         Zipping

words
always spill
from my mouth
and then
I'm trying
to shove them
back inside.

A HUGE Question

It's term break.
Five free days.
No school
to keep me
and my brain
busy.
I need busy
to stop my brain
from constantly thinking
about America
and Daddy,
and this one
nagging question.

WHEN ARE WE LEAVING?

Officer Graham keeps us busy

with a game of Skittles.
We have two teams.
Maggie and me.
Anna and Mark.
It's Officer Graham's game
from when he was a kid.
I'm up.
We're tied.
I need to knock down all nine wooden bottles
for Maggie and me to win.
I get three shots.

    Come on, Viva, Maggie cheers. *You can do it!*

        Winning team gets a box of Maltesers.
        Officer Graham waves the red box.

I love those chocolatey,
melt-in-your-mouth,
malted milk balls.
I grip the cheese tightly.
Not real cheese.
That would be gross.
This is a round, flat disc.
I aim at the bottles.

    *Do you know that it is 3,459 miles to fly from
London to New York?*
    Mark tells Anna.

THROW.
Five skittles down.
Maggie cheers!
She hands me another cheese.

    *It is 3,290 nautical miles if you go by sea and
that would take around 20 days.*

We're not going to New York by ship, Anna says.
We are definitely flying.

THROW.
Three skittles down.

> Maggie jumps and yells.
> *Just one more and we win!*
> She gives me the cheese.
> *Think of the Maltesers.*

I can do this!

> Come on, Viva,
> Officer Graham cheers.

Yummy malted chocolate.

> *Flying is one of the most expensive ways of travel,*
> Mark starts up again.
> *You wouldn't have to pay if HIAS sponsors you.*
> *I looked them up. It stands for Hebrew Immigrant*
> *Aid Society.*
> *If they don't help you, then you're kind of stuck.*

All I can hear is Mark.
His words are riling up
my insides.
SHHHH!

> *I don't think HIAS is helping us,* Anna says.

> *Too bad. Your plane tickets will cost a lot.*
> *I think you and Viva are going to be here a long time.*

THROW.
I miss.
Stupid Mark and Anna.

Later that night

Anna hands me
five Maltesers she saved and
a package wrapped
in faded, brown paper.

What's this?
I ask.

Open it.

I rip off the paper.
No way!
It's my wordbook.
I flip through it.
All the pages
I ripped out
are neatly taped
back together.

I know how much this book means to you.

I grab Anna
into a tight-sister hug
and squeeze.
I can't believe you put my book back together.
Thank you!

I have the perfect word for you to add, too.

Flibbertigibbet.

What's that?
It describes Maggie and actually, Mark too.

FLIBBERTIGIBBET: flib·ber·ti·gib·bet /ˈflibərdēˈjibət/
a person who talks incessantly

Postcard

Dear Anna and Viva,
I miss you and can't wait to show you
the sites of New York.
Love you both to bits,
Daddy

I trace Daddy's handwriting
on the back of the card,
my fingertip looping
    around the o
        flying up the V.

Stop!
Anna snatches the card from me.
You're going to smudge it.

I don't get mad.
I am filled up
with oodles of happiness.
    I'm going to
        see
            Daddy
                again.

Under the bed

I find
a missed torn paper
from my wordbook.

PATIENCE

> **PATIENCE: pa·tience /pāSHəns/**
> the capacity to accept or tolerate delay, trouble,
> or suffering without getting angry or upset

It's a message
from Daddy.
He's telling me
to wait.
Be patient.
It's hard when
all I want is
to be
a family again.
Daddy,
Mummy,
Anna,
and me.
TOGETHER.
I'm not
good at
being
patient.

The Grownups' Plan

When are we going to New York?
I ask Mummy.

> The tickets cost a lot of money.

I remember what Mark told Anna.
Dread creeps down my spine.
A week, two weeks, a month?

> Your daddy and I are saving to buy tickets so
> the three of us can fly together.

So how long?

Mummy lowers her head.

> It may take a while.

Fresh tears threaten to spill
and she wipes them away
with the back of her hand.

I can see that
Mummy's heart
is also heavy
from the waiting,
from all of the
feelings of missing Daddy.
I stop asking.

Mrs. Robinson tells me . . .

Patience is a virtue.
Good things come to those who wait.
I hate when grownups talk
in code.

April 1973

When
I
think
of
America

Easter Sunday

This Sunday,
we're combining two kitchens.
Indian and British.
It's Mummy and Mrs. Robinson's idea.
The menu . . .
Indian spiced beef roast.
Cumin roasted potatoes.
English peas.
Yorkshire pudding. (Mrs. Robinson's specialty, which
isn't pudding at all.)
Baath, or as Granny called it in Portuguese, *Bolo de
rulao* (my favorite cake.)

Mrs. Robinson's tiny kitchen
is brimming with . . .
sizzling onions and garlic,
smoky cumin and coriander,
fat green pods, waiting to be shelled,
a whirring blender,
lots of laugher,
giggling,
chatting,
and nibbling.

A feast of togetherness to make our taste buds dance.
I hope Daddy isn't alone.
Mark said Jewish people
don't celebrate Easter.
I wonder what
he's doing.
Daddy would
have loved our feast,
especially the *Bolo de rulao*.
It's his favorite too.

Serendipity

When I sneak
downstairs
for another piece
of baath,
I overhear Mummy
tell Mrs. Robinson
that HIAS is
going to sponsor us.
They will pay
for two tickets.
And here's the best part—
she and Daddy almost
have enough money saved
for a third ticket.

Fireworks light up
inside me.
I race upstairs
to tell Anna.
Then, stop.
Patience.
This is Mummy's news.
I will wait for her
to tell us.

Diana Ross,
Get ready,
Viva is coming to America.

When I think of America,

I think of a place where I'll . . .

be heard,
be seen,
be wanted in a way that feels safe,
be the kind of happy-exhausted from sleepovers
with friends.

When I think of America,
I think of Daddy and
the big, brilliant life
that is waiting
for us,
waiting
for
me.

I can't hold it in any longer.

Over fish and chips
in the MESS,
giddy and bubbling,
I tell Maggie my news.

I'm leaving for New York soon.

Maggie is silent.
Her usually smiley mouth
turns upside down,
hanging long.
I don't want you to go.
You're my best friend.

It will be okay.
I'll come back here.
And you can visit me
in New York.

I guess.
But it won't be the same.

I bite into my fish,
but it's hard to make it
go down my throat.
I don't say anything.
Maggie's right.
It won't
be
the
same.

Chaos in the MESS

At another table
a heated discussion
grows louder.
Words fly
at me,
around me,
surrounding me.

MONDAY CLUB   REPATRIATION

REPEAL RACE RELATIONS ACT—send them back!

HALT IMMIGRATION

They can't do this.
We have rights.
We have British passports.
They can't send us back.
Where will we go?

Feelings
   erupt
      around me.

Officer Graham appears
with another police officer
and motions for
Maggie and me
to wait outside.

Being Chased

REPATRIATION

HALT IMMIGRATION

SEND THEM HOME

chase after me
as Maggie and I
make our escape.
Loud.
Booming.
Scary.
WORDS.
I wish my WINGS
could unfurl
and sweep me
up and away
into the skies
all the way
across
the Atlantic Ocean
into Daddy's
safe arms.

UGLY New Word

The second I get home,
I flip through the
pages of Mini-Blue
until I find it.

REPATRIATION: re·pa·tri·a·tion /rē,pātrē'āSH(ə)n /
the return of someone to their own country

I don't understand
WHY.
Why they hate us.
Why they want us to leave.
Why they are so mean.
WHY?
Is there something wrong with us?

Will it be like this in America, too?

A Conversation with Mrs. Robinson After Supper

Why do they hate us?
I ask Mrs. Robinson as she hands me a wet plate to
dry.

Who?

I point to the front page of the *Daily Telegraph*.
At the photo of the picketers holding signs.
NO MORE ASIANS.

I don't know. They are ignorant.
And that's okay?

No!
Her voice has the force of a thunderstorm.
What happened to you in Southall was awful.
What the National Front and protestors are doing is wrong.
You should never be made to feel less for being YOU.

I rub the plate
until all
the wetness is gone.
If only it was as easy
to rub away my hurt.

Mrs. Robinson tosses the newspaper into the bin.
Viva, there are many British people that want you here.
They feel terrible about what the Asians from Uganda
are going through. People like Leroy and Officer Graham.

And you?

Oh, most definitely me.

And suddenly
I'm swallowed by a
HUGE squeeeezy tight,
English lavender-smelling
HUG.

271

It's never a good thing

when the telephone rings
in the middle
of the night.

So when Mummy walks
into our bedroom
and says,

Your father was in a car accident.

It's like a bomb
explodes,
shattering
my life
into a million little pieces.

Darkness

I can't sleep.
My tummy aches.
My happiness
is gone
leaving a big void.
Mummy doesn't know
I overheard her talking
to Mrs. Robinson
about flying to America.
What's going to happen now?
I'm trapped in
the empty space with
no sun,
no rainbows,
no hope
and it feels like
I'll never get out.
Never see Daddy again.

After School

The last time
I sat in this oak tree,
I was praying to God
to keep Daddy safe
and bring him to England
so I wouldn't have
to go to Southall.

He didn't hear me.

Maybe it's because
Officer Graham made
me climb down.
I think the higher up you are,
the closer to heaven,
God hears you better.

>   Dear God,
>   Please keep Daddy safe.
>   I will do anything.
>   I'll be patient,
>   listen to Mummy,
>   be thoughtful.
>   use kind words.
>   I will do anything.
>   ANYTHING!
>   Please.
>   Keep him safe
>   until Mummy, Anna,
>   and I get there.

Sobs gather in my throat,
I choke on the last few words.

Please, don't let Daddy die.

Mummy Is Disappearing

Mummy missed
supper
again today.
That's two days
where she's
stayed
in her room.

We need her.
Feisty Kampala Mummy
Maybe all Mummy's
courage
is used up
from being here
alone without Daddy.
From moving to Southall.
From flying bricks.
From long hours at Grunwicks.
From trying to protect Anna and me from hate.
Maybe Mummy's courage well
                      is
                  DRY.

Masala Chai

I know
what Mummy
needs
to soothe her
sadness
and ease
her worries.
    A
       cup
          of
            LOVE.

It's Daddy's specialty drink.
Masala Chai.
Love and sunshine
in a mug.
He makes it when
we're sad,
we're sick,
we're celebrating.
It's what he'd make
for Mummy if he were here.

Mrs. Robinson
lights the gas cooker
and helps Anna and me
make the fragrant tea.
Warm milk.
Black tea.
Sweet honey.
Earthy cardamom.
And a pinch
of shimmering sunshine.
Turmeric.
A cup of love.

Darkness

The dimly lit room
feels heavy
under the weight
of Mummy's sadness.

Anna goes inside.
I follow,
afraid to look.
Afraid of what
I will see.
Wanting to help,
but not
knowing
how.

Deu borem korum.
Mummy thanks us.
She breathes in
the fragrant spirals
of chai curling
around her mouth
and nose.
Her eyes well
with tears.

She squeezes
my hand
and warmth
flows
from her fingers
into mine.

Daddy Update

God
heard me.
Daddy isn't going to die.
He has broken bits . . .
Leg.
Ribs.
Arm.
But he isn't going to die.
THANK YOU,
God.

Under the Moon

The night air
has that damp
musty smell
that's become
familiar.
I'm sandwiched
between Maggie and Anna.
The stars glitter
overhead.
Mark hunts
for the Big Dipper.

> Once I find Polaris, the North Star,
> I can find the Big Dipper.

I shiver
and cross my arms
tightly
against my chest.
A storm is coming.
I tilt my head back.
The crescent moon
is etched
into the sky.
We've been here
almost eight months.
I think of Mummy.
Everything she's gone through,
everything she's done,
all out of love.
Love for us.
I didn't see it before.
I see it now.

Light

The answer
comes to me
so clear,
   so strong,
bright as the North Star
that I'm
surprised
I didn't think
of it sooner.

We have two tickets from HIAS.

Mummy and Anna should go to New York.

I Share My Brilliant Idea

What about you? Anna asks.

I'll stay here with Mrs. Robinson.

Alone?

I'll have Maggie and Mark, Officer Graham, and Leroy.

*You're crazy if you think Mummy's going to
leave you behind.*

It's just until they save up for another ticket.
If Mummy goes, she can help Daddy get better
faster.

Aren't you scared to stay here without us?

A little, but I'm trying not to think about it too
much. Diana Ross went out on her own.

You're not Diana Ross. You're ten.

I scowl at Anna.
I should have told Maggie first.

When I tell Maggie

my plan,
her scream is
so loud,
so piercing,
I know
she LOVES it.

When I tell Leroy
his dimples double wink.
Now that's some super-duper
SUPREMENESS!
he tells me.
Your daddy sure will be proud.

When I tell Mark
he's gobsmacked!

When I ask Mrs. Robinson
she says,
ABSOLUTELY
I can stay with her
and she gathers me
into one of her
too-tight smothering hugs.
I let her.

Telling Mummy

Mummy sits outside
marking papers.
I remember
what Leroy's mum
told him.
That you get
courage
by doing small things,
one at a time.
I slip my hand
inside my pocket
and squeeze my WINGS
for good luck.

I walk outside
and join Mummy
on the steps.

　　Mummy?

　　Hmmmmm?

　　I have an idea.

　　What's that?

Deep breath.
In and out.
Here I go . . .

I heard you and Mrs. Robinson talking. HIAS
gave us two plane tickets.
You and Anna should go to New York. Anna
is still recovering from her
meningitis. Daddy needs you. We can't wait.
You and Anna have to go.

I say it super duper fast.
Then wait.
Mummy doesn't say anything.
Did she hear me?

She looks up
and cups my face
with loving hands.

My darling girl,
all you've wanted since we arrived in England is to
see your dad.

But right now, he needs you more than I need him.
I feel the tears pooling in my eyes.

I can't leave you here alone.

She won't be alone.
Mrs. Robinson stands in the doorway.
She'll be with me.

I take another breath and gather more courage.
My mind is made up.
You and Anna should go.

Mummy thrums her fingers
against the stack
of papers
in her lap
and my heart
beats in rhythm.
    Yes?
    No?
    Maybe?
    What will it be?
I hold my breath.
Waiting.

        I'll think about it and talk to Daddy.

I fling my arms
around Mummy.
Papers scatter.
We fall backward
laughing,
arms wrapped
around one
another
        tightly.

Term Break

Leroy got me a job
during term break.
I'm helping sort the post
coming from America
and going to America.

I can save money
for my plane ticket.
AND
buy all the Maltesers
I want.

    I'm still waiting for Mummy
    to say YES to my idea.
    What is taking her so long?
    It's been over a week.
    Maybe Daddy said NO.

      Patience, Viva.

Three Days Later

Mummy is waiting
for me when I get home.
She talked to Daddy.
And I can't BELIEVE it.
He said YES.
It's probably because
he really needs Mummy.

> *You've given me such joy.*
> *Mummy beams with pride.*
> *You remind me of your grandmother.*
> *You have her spirit.*

> > *And temper, too?*
> > *Anna throws in, with a giggle.*
> > *I've heard Gran shouting at Papa.*

A hint
of a smile
appears
on Mummy's face
and my head
and heart
know
I'm doing
the right
thing.

May 1973

Cool
like
Diana
Ross

Things Go Wrong

I have to fly
to New York
with
   Wait for it . . .
     Meena Auntie and Sanjeev.
The thing is,
you have to be fourteen
to fly from London
to New York
unaccompanied—
that's without an adult.

Mummy was going to cancel the whole trip.
But then, Meena Auntie said she was flying to New York
to visit her sister and would take me.
Mummy just has to get the money for my ticket by
the end of June.
That's when Meena Auntie is going to New York.

Mummy asked if I was okay with the new plan
and I wanted to say NOOOOOO,
but her eyes were so full of hope and pleading
and I really want to do this for her and Daddy,
so I said YES.

Now all I can think about is that flight.
What if I have to sit with Sanjeev?
I remember his smelly room.
The average person
farts five to fifteen
times per day.
I learned that
from Mark.

I will be flying
in a fart cloud.

Aghhhhh!

Helping Anna Pack

Viva?
Yup.

Thanks for letting me go to New York with Mum.
You've got those leftover meningitis cooties. I need
you far away from me.

Seriously. You're a pretty cool sister.
Cool like Diana Ross.

I've always been a little jealous.
Of Diana?

No silly. You.
Really?

*I wish I were more like you—brave. I read about
adventures. You make them happen.*
I think you're pretty brave with all of the yucky
health stuff you deal with.

It's not the same.
I wish I was more like you, especially when I get
angry and my lava mouth takes over. That never
happens to you. Mummy and Daddy count on you
to do the right thing.

I'm boring.
Nope. You're dependable. It would be boring if we
were exactly the same.

You're a great sister.
I know you are going to really, really, really miss me.
I know you are going to really, really, really miss me!

You'll miss me more.
WRONG! You will.

Anna flies across the room,
and lands on top of me.
Ow!
We fall back onto the bed,
giggling and hugging.

On the way to the airport

Mummy tells me
how proud
she is of me.
Then she cries
and keeps asking
if I'm okay
and worrying
that I'm not.

Anna gives me
a super-duper
squeezy-tight sister hug
and says
I'm just like
one of the Adventurous Five
from her Enid Blyton books.

Suddenly all these
missing-them
feelings are growing
inside me
and Mummy and Anna
haven't even left yet.
I have to make them
STOP.

What have I done?

A tight lump forms in my throat
as Anna and I follow
Mummy and Mrs. Robinson
to the departure gate.
I can't help thinking that
this is just like when we left Daddy
at the airport in Uganda and he said
he'd see us in five days.

FLIGHT 764 to New York City boarding now!

A tornado of panic and worry whirls inside me.

What if something happens and I'm stuck
in England?
What if I never ever see Daddy, Mummy, and
Anna again?
What if I have to live with Mrs. Robinson forever?

I can't breathe.
Don't go! Don't leave me, I want to shout.

Anna intertwines her fingers with mine.
She squeezes my hand.

*Two months, she says. May and June. You'll be in
New York in no time. You'll see.*

But all I can think is
that two months
is an eternity.

Suddenly,
the tears that I haven't cried
in the weeks leading up
to this day
finally break free
in great big sobs.

Mummy rushes over
and pulls me into one of
her squeeeezy tight hugs
and doesn't let go
until every last sob
is hugged out of me.

Final boarding for FLIGHT 764 to New York City!

Mummy has
to get on the flight,
but she doesn't move.
She cups my face
in her hands
and looks me
straight in the eyes.

> I promise, Viva. Two months. No more. You'll see
> us in two months.

I swallow,
take a deep gulpy breath,
nod and
SLOWLY
step back.
        You better go, I tell her.

Mrs. Robinson lays her hands
on my shoulders
and I lean against her.
The second Mummy and Anna
walk through the gate,
I rush to the window,
waving wildly
when they appear on the tarmac.
Mummy smiles and waves back.
Anna waves nonstop
until she disappears
inside the plane.
And only when the plane
is no bigger than a spec of dust,
do I turn to Mrs. Robinson.

                    I'm ready now.

The days tumble

into one another,
helping ease
my missing
and wishing I
was with
Mummy,
Anna,
and especially
         DADDY.

That One Big Question

Ever since
I found out we
are going to New York,
there's been one question
niggling me.

Is America like Britain?

It is causing me
massive, persistent, agonizing
WORRY!

NIGGLING: niggling /ˈnigliNG/
causing slight but persistent annoyance, discomfort,
or anxiety

There's only one American

I trust to tell me the truth.
Leroy.
I ask him while we're
sorting the post.

> Are Americans like the British?
> Leroy hands me a stack of letters.
> *What do you mean?*

> Do they like people like us?
> *You mean Supreme-singing, Motown-loving,*
> *boogie-bopping people?*

> No. I smile, and then get serious. I mean brown people.
> Leroy pats a stool and I climb up.
> *Viva, there are always gonna be people that judge.*
> *You could be too tall, too short, too skinny, too fat,*
> *light, dark, pink, or green.*

> Green?
> *You haven't seen my Uncle Earl after too many*
> *slices of Mamma's pie.*
> *Green as a frog.*
> *But there are whole bunches of other people that*
> *will look at you. And they . . .*

> Will see me?
> *Yup!*
> *They will see YOU and all your fabulous Supremeness.*
> *You can't let the haters get you down, Viva.*
> *Spread those WINGS and SOAR above the hate.*
> *Don't let anyone make you feel LESS for being YOU.*

They call you names, you tell them . . .

"STOP! In the Name of Love."

Better yet, sing it LOUDLY.

I jump off the stool and sing, adding all the moves,
just like Diana Ross.

Girl Guides Brownie Badges

You have to help me!
Maggie announces.
And then,
before I can ask anything,
she is off,
feet moving
up and down the stairs,
in and out of her bedroom,
around the dining table,
flopping on and off the settee.

*I was supposed to be working on cooking and my
hostess stuff and THIS!*
She waves a ball of yarn and knitting needles.
*I can't be the only one not getting their badges.
What will Troop Leader Luiza say?
No. No. No. This can't be happening.
There's no way I can do everything in two days.*

I can't keep up with Maggie.
Stop!
I hold my hands up
like Diana Ross.
What's going on?

She was supposed to finish a bunch of stuff
to earn her Girl Guide badges
and, classic Maggie, left it until the last minute,
Mark says.

You're not helping. Maggie glares at Mark. What am
I going to do? she wails.

I'll help, I tell her.

Really?

I nod.

Maggie squeals and jumps
up and down
like a pogo stick.

BUSY Bee Brownies

My fingers
are knotted,
cramped claws from
too much knitting,
but we did it!
Maggie and me.
Four squares each.
Some dropped stitches.
A little crooked.
Eight knitted squares.
   Knitting badge earned.

While Mrs. Robinson
sews the knitted squares
into a scarf,
Maggie pours hot water
into the teapot and I
arrange biscuits
on a plate.
We serve Mrs. Robinson.
   Hostess badge earned.

Potatoes cubed.
Onions chopped.
Pinch of . . .
turmeric, salt, pepper,
and curry powder.
Tossed and roasting in the oven.
   Cooking badge earned.

I couldn't have done this without you,
Maggie says while we wash up.
She flicks soapy water at me.
I flick soapy suds back at her.
She squeals.
We laugh.
But a little part of me
wishes Anna was with us.

June 1973

I

miss

you

soooo

much.

Letter from Anna

Dear Viva,

I can't believe it's been one whole month since we left England.

I miss you *sooooo* much.

We all do, especially now that Daddy is home from the hospital.

I can't wait until you get here. You are going to LOVE it. We don't exactly live in New York. We're in Pennsylvania. It's a different state.

They have fifty of them. FIFTY. We're going to need Mark's brain to remember them all.

Our flat is in Scranton and it's lovely. Not like that ugly one Meena Auntie sent us to in Southall. You'll really like it here.

There are . . .
    No angry picketers.
    No flying bricks.
    No mean people.

There is one weird thing. Are you ready for this? We're the only brown people in the whole city.

THE ONLY ONES!

Sometimes when we're out people give us curious glances and sideway looks. I think of you and channel your inner Diana Supremeness and give them my own funny face. That usually makes them stop.

I have good news, which you will probably already know by the time this letter gets to you, but anyway . . . I heard Daddy and Mummy whispering last night about money. I know it's about your ticket. I couldn't hear everything, but I think you'll be coming here SOON.

They said something about flying with Meena Auntie, which has to mean that they have the money. You'll be here at the end of the month.

That's not too long.

Three to four weeks, depending on when you get this letter.

Eat lots of fish and chips before you get here.

HUGE sister hugs.
Anna

p.s. So sorry you have to fly with Sanjeev.
p.p.s. Say hello to Maggie and Mark.

There's an ocean distance

between Daddy and me
but Mummy and Anna's closeness
to him,
feels like his hugging arms
are almost
touching me
and soon
I will be giving
him great big
HUGS
in person.

The Telegram

June 06, 1973

We miss you, Viva. Good news! You are
flying with Meena Auntie on June 28th.
We will wire the money so Mrs. Robinson
can buy your ticket.
Can't wait to see you.
        Love Mummy, Daddy, and Anna

Me? A Brownie.

Here, put this on.
Maggie thrusts a brown dress and yellow tie at
me.

What is it?

*Your Brownie uniform. You're coming with me to the
troop meeting. I told Troop Leader Luiza how you
helped me and how you stayed back so your mum and
Anna could go to New York to help your dad and she
said you are the perfect Girl Guide and could be an
honorary member until you fly to New York. She gave
me the uniform for you to wear.*

I try to keep up with Maggie
as words fly out of her mouth.

*Well, don't just stand there.
HURRY!!!*

Maggie doesn't need
to tell me twice.
I race upstairs.

As Maggie and I
skip-walk to the church
where the troop meetings
are held,
I can't help
wondering if
I'll get a badge.
I hope so.

And guess what?
I do.

Three badges:
Cooking,
Friendship,
and Singer
for
my
Diana Ross Supremeness.
Plus
Book Lover—a badge for Anna.

It was all Maggie's idea.
I just know that Anna will
love the badge
And I can't wait to give it to her.

No More Fish and Chips at the MESS

RAF Greenham resettlement camp
is getting ready to close
at the end of the month.
The same time that
I am leaving England.

Maggie, Mark, and I
are helping with the
clean up and clear out.
Old Mrs. Robinson is back!

> Sheets into the bags.
> Move those mattresses.
> Gather those towels.

Officer Graham is here
with other police.
Leroy is here
with other airmen.
All traces
of the Indians
who stopped here
are being erased
little by little.

My memories are tucked
in and around every corner.

Meeting Maggie and Mark in the common room.
Building Guy Fawkes and our bonfire.
Feeling suffocated in the too-full barracks.
Praying with Officer Graham under the oak tree.
Dancing and singing with Leroy.

And my FAVORITE . . .

Eating fish and chips for the very first time!

Fifteen Days and Counting

Mrs. Robinson got all
of the flight details
from Meena Auntie.

Now we just need
the money. It's been
a week and nothing.
Maybe wiring money
takes a long time.

   (*Note to self:* ASK MARK.)

I can't believe
that I'll be standing
on the same continent as
Diana Ross
in exactly fifteen days.

Someday we'll be together . . . Daddy, Mummy, Anna,
and me.
Yes we will.

I throw out my arms and sing loudly.

Movie Night with the RAF Gang

Robin Hood is playing.
We fill almost a whole row in the cinema.
Maggie, Mark, and me.
Officer Graham and his boys.
Yes, Officer Graham is a dad.
Who knew?

Leroy and
    wait for it . . .
        Miss Robinson.
They are dating.
And, right behind them,
with watching eyes,
are Mrs. Robinson and Mrs. Mackay.

We eat popcorn.
Watch Robin Hood outsmart Prince John.
Sing along to "Oo-De-Lally"
and giggle
when Leroy and Miss Robinson hold hands.
I can't wait to tell Anna.

On the way home,
Maggie and I sing
"Oo-De-Lally".
Our own version . . .

Maggie and Viva walkin' through the forest
Laughin' back and forth at what Mark has to say
Reminiscin', this-'n'-that in' havin' such a good time
Oo-de-lally, oo-de-lally, golly, what a day

Maggie and Mark

come over after school.
While Mark reads
his science magazine,
Maggie and I
paint our toenails,
picking different colors
for each toe.

What's wrong? I ask Maggie. You're not talking.
Nothing.

Is it the test for your Girl Guide Wilderness
badge?
No.

Did Rude Ruth make fun of your potato toes
at swimming?
Maggie shakes her head.

Then what?
Nothing.

Mark peers over his magazine.
You're leaving in two weeks and she doesn't want
you to go.

Maggie's eyes water.
The
dam
breaks . . .

Maggie Madness

It's too awful.
What am I going to do without you?
  Oomph.
  I'm attacked by skinny arms and knobby elbows.

You're such a great friend.
And I'm awful.
Mark said all that stuff about Southall being a
purple city.
  Red city, Mark corrects her.

Right. Red city.
And I left you there all alone and then I stapled your
letter to my math homework. I'm the worst friend.
I should have asked Mummy if you could stay with me
right from the beginning.

  Her too-tight arms squeeze my breath.
  She's in full FLIBBERTIGIBBET mode.
  There's no stopping her.

I didn't get it . . . didn't understand what it was like
for you.
You being brown and the NF and mean kids.
I don't blame you if you never want to see me again.
No, that's a lie.
You have to keep in touch after you leave.
Write.
Promise to visit.
Please. Please. Please.

  MAGGIE!

What?
    You're a GREAT friend.
    You made being in England okay.
    You're SUPREME!
        Oomph.
        Skinny arms and knobby elbows attack.
            Again.

When Mrs. Robinson gets home

I immediately know something is wrong.
Let's sit down. Your parents sent another
telegram.
I don't want to sit. Just tell me.

I'm sorry, luv, your parents need you to stay with
me a little bit longer.
I don't understand. Mummy said I'd be flying to
New York with Meena Auntie and Sanjeev. They
were wiring the money for my ticket.

Viva, they weren't expecting the hospital bills.
What does that have to do with me flying to
New York?

The money they'd saved for your ticket was used
to pay the medical bills for your father.
What about me?

Well, school in America starts in September and—
SEPTEMBER! They're leaving me here until
September?

They are hoping to have the money by the end of
August so you can start school on time.
But that's another two months away.

They miss you and are doing everything they can.
I miss them.

I know you do.

That's when I finally
sit next to Mrs. Robinson
and she wraps her arms around me
squeezing out all of
the disappointment
and the sadness
and the anger
until I can't hold them
in any longer
and they burst,
pouring out of me
in a flood
of tears.

Gloom and Doom

When we first got
to the resettlement camp
Mummy and Anna
were full of gloom
and doom.
All the sun
had been
squeezed out
of them
and there was
nothing left
but sadness.

It was up to me
to spark the sunshine
and keep it lit.

Now my life
is all gloom
and doom.

Since Mrs. Robinson told
me the news about
staying with her
until September,
everyone's been trying
to light my spark
with trips to London,
afternoon movies,
and visits to the seaside,
but it's not enough
to spark my sunshine
and keep it glowing.

Not when the hurt
and missing
and disappointment
is too much.

June 28th, 1973

I was supposed
to fly
to New York today.

Meena Auntie and Sanjeev
are on the plane
somewhere over the Atlantic ocean.

I'm in Newbury, England.

July 1973

Someone

like

me.

Someone Like Me

While waiting
at the park
for Maggie
          I see her.
A brown girl,
like me.
Loneliness,
uncertainty,
and fear
are wrapped
around her
like a pashmina scarf.
I know
because I
wore
that same scarf
not too long ago.

Uma

I sit on the swing beside her.
She looks up.
Surprised.
> Hi. I'm Viva.
> *I'm Uma.*

> Did you just move here?
> She nods.
> Give it time, I tell her. It will get better.

She shakes her head.
> *I don't belong here. They don't want me.*
> *I'm just another Paki.*

That's not true.
You belong wherever you want to be.
You can't give up.

> *I'm too scared. I can't make people like me.*
> *I can't change what I look like . . . my skin color.*

I promise there are people that want you here.
They will see YOU.
I can tell Uma doesn't believe me.
I look at my WINGS.
I show them to Uma and tell her their story.
> They helped me soar above the fear and hate
> to find my place here.

> *Can I hold them?*

Uma runs her finger
along the edge of each wing tip.
She takes a deep breath.
Her shoulders straighten,
just a little.

I look at Uma and
wonder if it's time to free
my wings so they
can help someone else.
I'd like to think they
could help her just like
they helped me.

I hear my name and look up.
Maggie is charging toward us.

> Sorry I'm late. Mark has the house key and took
> FOREVER at the library.
> I was standing outside our house for at least
> fifteen minutes doing the wee
> dance. I thought I was going to pee my pants.

I glance at Uma.
She's got the same
look I probably had
on my face the first time
I met Maggie.

SHOCK!

She'll stop soon,
I whisper.
Uma softly giggles
and Maggie stops.

Who's your new friend?

This is Uma.

Hi Uma. I'm Maggie. I—

Maggie is cut off
by someone waving
and calling to Uma.

That's my brother. I've got to go.
Here!

She holds out my wings.
I take a deep breath.
Keep them!

Really?

Yup!

Thank you!
Uma's eyes light up.

That glow
pushes my gloom out
and sparks my sunshine.
I look at Maggie
and hope she and Uma will become friends.

Leroy

OH, MY GOD! (*Sorry God for taking your name in vain, but this news is HUGE*)

I'm flying
to New York in
        one week.
        Seven days.
        One hundred sixty-eight hours.
STOP!
How did Mark get inside my head?

Leroy got permission
to take a civilian—
what Air Force people
call people not in the Air Force—
on his next flight to America.
I'll be flying with the sacks of post
across the Atlantic to New York City.

He didn't want to tell me
until he knew for sure.
At first his boss said NO.
But after Leroy explained
everything,
he changed his mind
and AGREED.
He already sent a message
to Daddy and Mummy
and they gave permission.

One week.
Seven days.
One hundred sixty-eight hours . . .

STOP!
Mark Mackay, get out of my brain!

Seven days take forever when you

are counting
the hours,
the minutes,
the seconds
of every single day.

Or trying
to decide what
to pack
and what
to leave behind.

And spending
as much time
as possible with
friends because
you're scared
you'll never
see them
again.

Seven days
takes forever
when you're
wavering between
an end
and a
brand
new
beginning.

And then suddenly

they are up
and it's my last night
here and I'm curled
on the settee
with Mrs. Robinson.
We sip masala chai,
watching the rain
pitter-patter
on the window,
thinking about
the first day
she shushed my
Diana Supremeness
with her red-tipped finger
and how she is now
one of my Supremes.

I'm too excited to sleep.

I lay in bed
staring out the window
and think about
the past ten months,
the ugly words flung at me.
    Paki,
    Brown Monkey

I know I won't ever be
what some people
think is perfect . . .
    White skin.
    Blonde or brown braids.
    Light colored eyes.

It's okay.
Brown is beautiful.
Diana Ross and the Supremes
are brown and they
are beautiful.
I am who I am . . .
    An Indian girl, with brown skin, and black hair.

ALIVE   SPIRITED   BRAVE
BROWN   BEAUTIFUL

I won't let anyone make me feel bad for being ME.

I will be
the best of
ME.
I can.

Get ready, America!
Viva's on her way.

I Hate Goodbyes

I've planned this day
in my head
for so long
that I can picture
the whole thing.
Getting on the jet.
Flying across the Atlantic Ocean.
Seeing the Statue of Liberty from the sky.
Stepping off the plane into Daddy's arms.

The only thing I can't imagine
is leaving behind my new friends.
    Mrs. Robinson.
    Maggie.
    Mark.
    Officer Graham.
    Miss Robinson.

I don't know how to say it.
                    Goodbye.
There are no magic words.
There's no right way.
I have no words.
But I have HUGS,
        Thank-you hugs,
        Promise-to-write-letter hugs,
        Never-ever-forget-you hugs,
        Ever-so-tight squeeezy hugs.

When I'm all hugged out,
I wipe my tears
and with one final last look
at my friends,
I turn and climb
into the jet.

Sitting in the Cockpit

I'm sitting right up front with Leroy
surrounded by
    weird dials,
    speedometers,
    and gauges.
I have no idea what they do.
Mark would know.

The inside of the jet
is smaller than the plane
I flew in from Kampala
to London.

A LOT SMALLER.

I sing a little Supremes
to help ease my fears,
but Diana doesn't seem
to work today.

So instead, I think
of how many times
Leroy has flown
from America to London
from London to America
and not once has he fallen
out of the sky.
Seven hours.
That's how long it takes
to get to New York.
Leroy buckles me in.

    Okay, co-pilot. Ready to fly?

    Yessir.
    I give him two thumbs up.

Takeoff

We're moving.
Sputtering down the airstrip.
Rolling over the bumpy ground.
Slowly gaining speed.
The jet propellers
spin into a
deafening roar.
We're moving fast.
Any minute now,
the nose
is going to lift
toward the sky.
I clench my fists tightly.
Hold my breath.
My body tilts
toward the sun
and we fly upward
to dance with the clouds.

Below me I see
the barracks where I lived when we were on base,
the MESS, where I tasted my first fish and chips,
the common room where I met Maggie and Mark.

Sky, then ground.
Then, sky and ground.
My friends
get smaller and smaller
until they are no bigger than ants.

Goodbye, RAF Greenham.
Goodbye, England.
Goodbye, Queen Elizabeth.

I SOAR

on silver wings
high above the clouds
into an endless sea of blue
to DADDY,
   MUMMY,
      and ANNA.

Seven Hours Later

We dip down.
Fuzzy browns, grays, and blues change
into rivers,
and lots of TALL buildings.
There she is!
Lady Liberty.
Standing so tall and straight.
Welcoming me to America.
        HELLO USA!
Leroy laughs.
    Hold on tight,
    he tells me.
    We're heading to the base.

The jet tilts and dips.
My stomach does the same.
A runway stretches before us like a long tongue.

    Grab the yoke and help me land.

I sit up straighter
and grip the steering
in both hands,
tightly.

    Keep your eyes on the runway.

That's all I'm doing.
I can't breathe.
We move down
    down
        down
            THUMP we land on the ground, zooming
            down the runway
and then STOP.

My American Airman

It's my one last
    GOODBYE
and it's for Leroy.

    Just remember Lil' Diana,
    Keep FLYING
    SOAR
    SHINE in all your Supremeness.

I promise.
One small step at a time.
He grins,
his eyes sparkle,
and he starts singing . . .

    "Someday We'll Be Together"

Yes sir!
I shout after him.

Leroy keeps walking,
grinning back at me
over his shoulder
just like he did
that first day
we met.

I see Mummy and Anna first

and right behind them
is Daddy,
his smile HUGE,
and arms open wide.

I'm bursting
full with all of my
missing, waiting, happiness feelings
pressing into my ribs and heart.
    I run.
        Feet racing.
            Heart beating.
                WINGS soaring
        straight into Daddy's arms.

DADDY. DADDY. DADDY

I say over and over,
hugging him
as tight as I can,
his stubbly chin tickling my cheek.

With his arms
Around me
Daddy sings a little Supremes.
    "Back in My Arms Again."

And I know sure as sure
that everything
is going to be all right.

I hug Daddy tighter,
Never wanting
To let go.

On the drive home

I fill Daddy in
on life in England.

Maggie's non-stop talking.
Mark's super-duper encyclopedia brain.
Leroy's wings.
Officer Graham saving us.
Mrs. Robinson in curlers and cold cream
scaring me and Anna
on our first night
at her place.

We all laugh.
Daddy,
Mummy,
Anna,
and me.

The sound feels
like love
like home.

After supper I take out my wordbook.

I show Daddy
Mini Blue and
all the words I collected
in England.

Words that brought us together.
Words that separated us.
Words that hurt my heart.
Words that tickled my insides.
And the best kind of words,
the ones that felt like a great big hug.

I show him the first word
I looked up when I got to England—**refugee**.

I hated the word because
of how others used it
and how it
made me feel.

Daddy kisses my forehead
easing the tiny bit
of hurt
lingering.

  I am so very proud of you!

He wraps his arms
around me
and we sit together,
looking at the moon
and the stars
and out
into the future,
waiting.
Our future.

That night,

I make Anna squeeze
into the top bunk
with me
so Daddy has
the bottom bunk.

Mummy doesn't mind,
  I'll have the whole bed to myself and nobody will
  be stealing the covers,
she says with a cheeky smile.

Daddy sits with us
until we fall asleep
just like he used to
when we lived
in Kampala
and then
I make him promise
to come back
and sleep with us.

I wake several times
during the night,
with Anna's arms
squeeeezy tight around me
and hang
over the edge
to check,
to make sure
Daddy is still there.
                    And
                    he
                    is.

342

Who Am I?

It's time
for a brand
new wordbook
for this new life
in this new country
and I know exactly
what word
I will start with.

I pull out my book,
open to the first page,
and write

> **VIVA:**
> Supremely fabulous.

That's me.

Author's Note

Although *Wings to Soar* is fictional, many of the situations Viva encounters are based on events that occurred in 1972, during a refugee crisis, when thousands of Ugandan Asians with British citizenship were arriving in the United Kingdom after being expelled from Uganda.

During this time, strong anti-immigration feelings were on the rise in the United Kingdom. Breaking away from the non-discriminatory immigration policy in place, Parliament had passed the Commonwealth Immigrant Act of 1968, which restricted the rights of British citizens living in Commonwealth countries and former colonies from migrating to the United Kingdom. Three years later the Immigrations Act of 1971 passed, imposing even further restrictions. The arrival of thousands of displaced Ugandan Asians fueled the anger and hatred within groups like the National Front, who held rallies and marches in protest of the immigration of non-whites.

I was six years old when President Idi Amin expelled Ugandan Asians from Uganda. We lived in London, and I have memories of family and friends staying with us before settling in the UK or emigrating on to Canada or the United States. I often wondered what it must have been like for those people who didn't have friends or family to stay with after leaving Uganda. What happened to them when they arrived in the UK? Where did they go? What did it feel like being in a country completely different from the one they'd left?

As I began the research for *Wings to Soar*, I stumbled on hidden golden nuggets. I learned that sixteen resettlement camps had been set up, and numerous volunteers from the Women's Royal Voluntary Service (WRVS) and Red Cross worked tirelessly to welcome and support the thousands of Ugandan Asians arriving in the UK.

One of those bases—RAF Greenham Common— was run by the United States Air Force. I imagined US airmen and Ugandan Asian refugees sharing a base. I don't know if their paths ever crossed, but I like to think some Ugandan Asian child felt less lonely because of a smiling, singing airman like Leroy. Through that same Facebook group, I met Mr. Graham Jewell, a police officer, who was stationed at RAF Greenham Common resettlement camp. For six weeks, he lived in the same accommodations as the refugees. His duties included ensuring the safety and security of the refugees and their belongings. He helped facilitate liaising with the British Immigration officials, took Ugandan Asians shopping, and helped introduce them to life in Britain. If you haven't guessed by now, Graham Jewell offered inspiration for the character of Officer Graham in my book.

Viva's supremeness is very much her own, but her story mirrors some of my own personal experiences.

Photographs

p. vi–1: Gate to Greenham Common, 1961/Creative Commons Attribution Share-alike license 2.0

p. 48–49: Jonathan Sayers/Greenham Common

p. 93: Bella Shannon/Illustration of wings, gift to Viva

p. 98–99: Tav Dulay/National Front march in Yorkshire, Great Britain, English Social Movement, GNU Free Documentation License

p. 138–139: Andrew Hackney/*King Street, Southall*/CC BY-SA 2.0, May 1981, Creative Commons Attribution Share-alike license 2.0

p. 186–187: Philip Halling/Geograph Britain and Ireland/City of Westminster/Whitehall, February 1974, Creative Commons Attribution Share-alike license 2.0

p. 220–221: Jonathan Sayers/Newbury

p. 262–263: Library of Congress/Prints and Photographs Division (reproduction number LC-USZ62-87844)

p. 288–289: GAC-General Artists Corporation-IMTI-International Talent Management Inc./public domain, photo of *The Supremes* in 1967

Pages 304–305: Jonathan Sayers/Newbury

Pages 322–323: Anonymous/public domain

SERENDIPITY: ser·en·dip·i·te /ˌserənˈdipəti/
occurring or discovering by chance in a happy
or beneficial way

Supremeness

EXPIRE: ex·pire /ikˈspī(ə)r/
to die, as a person

COLLYWOBBLES: col·ly·wob·bles /ˈkälēˌwäbəlz/
stomach pain or queasiness
Intense anxiety or nervousness

ALIVE

SPIRITED

FLIBBERTIGIBBET: flib·ber·ti·gib·bet /ˈflibərdēˈjibət/
a person who talks incessantly

Don't let anyone
make you feel LESS
for being YOU.

EXPIRE: ex·pire /ikˈspī(ə)r/
cease to be valid, as a document, authorization,
or agreement, typically after a fixed period of time